NOTHING IS FORGOTTEN

A COLLECTION OF KANPUR STORIES

akṣamālā

akṣamālā

Inknuts Multimedia Solutions Pvt. Ltd.

Mercury House, 1st Floor, 17/11 A, The Mall, Kanpur - 208001 Uttar Pradesh, India

First published in 2014 by Akṣamālā

Copyright © Inknuts Multimedia Solutions Pvt. Ltd., 2014

Cover Design: Mukul Khattar

Editor: Aprameya Manthena

All rights reserved

ISBN: 978-81-922539-3-0

Formatting and typesetting: Inknuts Multimedia Solutions Pvt. Ltd.

www.inknuts.com

Available from Amazon.com and other retail outlets Available on Kindle and other devices

This book is sold subject to the condition that it shall not by way of trade or otherwise, be lent, resold, hired out, circu- lated, and no reproduction in any form, in whole or in part (except for brief quotations in critical articles or reviews) may be made without written permission of the publishers.

For the people of Kanpur,

By the people of Kanpur

CONTENTS

- PREFACE •   I
- ABOUT KANPUR •   III

- THOSE WERE THE DAYS •   1
- KNOWING YOU •   8
- A BLISSFUL JOURNEY •   17
- CLOCK WORK •   23
- THE CAWNPORE OF YORE •   29
- THE STORY OF 'THE STORY-TELLER' •   34
- A CHILDHOOD TRAPPED •   43
- IRONY OF LIFE •   47
- THE CITY OF LOVE, LIFE & PASSION •   57
- LOVE THY CITY AS THY COMPANION •   63
- LOVE AT FIRST SIGHT •   74
- NOTHING IS FORGOTTEN •   82

- AUTHOR PROFILES •   85

• PREFACE •

This anthology is the culmination of Pen it Down Writing Awards 2013. As part of an initiative to encourage the love for reading and writing in the city of Kanpur, Inknuts Multimedia Solutions Pvt. Ltd. and The Katha Vidya Trust announced the awards in early 2013. We invited the residents of the city to write stories revolving around Kanpur.

The promise was to publish the best entries as an anthology *Nothing is Forgotten – a collection of Kanpur stories* under the imprint Aksamala (Inknuts' publishing wing). The contest evoked some curiosity and enquiries poured in. This was a positive sign for us to push as many residents to participate. Also, many demanded for the contest to be bilingual, given the Hindi speaking strength in the city. We are happy to share that a similar contest in Hindi is in the offing.

The idea behind this publication is to bring about feelings of love and ownership for Kanpur in the hearts of its residents. Over the years, while many cities have reached the helm of development, time has sort of stood still in Kanpur. The responsibility to change things for the better lies majorly with the owners, in this case the residents of the city. The stories include elements of love, wrath, warmth, anger, and innumerable aspects entwined with either a journey of childhood, finding love or coming back home to mum's cooking. Some have a sense of disappointment while others speak of hope. Overall, every story carries with it a freshness, a genuine sense of attachment to the city, and most importantly the hope for it to see a better tomorrow.

As for us, our job has just begun - the change is yet to come but the spark has been ignited.

Gautama Buddha had once said, ***"Words have power to destroy or heal, when words are both true and kind they can change our world."***

We at Inknuts truly believe every word in this collection has the power to bring the change we collectively dream of.

• ABOUT KANPUR •

Once upon a time, nestled on the banks of The Ganges, there was a city named Kanhiyapur. It was one of the main centres of industrial revolution in India. As time went by, the city was rechristened time and again. Some called it Kanhiyapur and fondly believed it to be the town of Kanhaiya or Lord Krishna, while others called it Karnapur, the town of Karna one of the heroes of Mahabharata. During the British rule, around the year 1776, Kanpur came to be known as Cawnpore.

The city boasts of a rich industrial heritage, beautifully demonstrated by the name Manchester of India. Only few know the integral role it played in the literary movements during the first half of the 20th century. It is believed that the first modern Indian novel 'Nashtar' was written in Kanpur by Hasan Shah. It was first published in Farsi in 1790, then translated into Urdu in 1893. It was then translated into English and renamed 'The Dancing Girl.'

Many acclaimed authors and poets in the past hailed from Kanpur. A popular shopping centre is named Navin Market, after the poet Bal Krishna Sharma "Navin". Later poets included Gopal Das "Niraj" who wrote songs for Hindi films. Kanpur is also the birthplace of Shyamlal Gupta 'Parshad', composer of the famous song *Vijayee Vishwa Tiranga Pyara.*

The propagation and popularisation of Hindi also owes much to this city, with great Hindu literatteurs such as Acharya Mahavir Parasad Dwivedi, Ganesh Shankar Vidyarthi, Pratap Narain Mishra and Acharya Gaya Prasad Shukla `Sanehi'.

Today, after a journey of 210 years, the city is known as Kanpur. Over the years, it has witnessed various transformations name wise, geographically, and culturally.

After this exhaustive journey, a lot has been discovered yet a lot remains unexplored. Today, the city craves for change, a better today and a brighter tomorrow. It dreams of encapsulating its rich heritage for its future generations. It wants to rid itself of the evil shadows of stagnation, pollution, poverty and political battles.

Today, it just wants to be able to breathe anew, just like the yesteryears...

• THOSE WERE THE DAYS •

AJAY MOHAN JAIN

My earliest memory of the city I adore dates back to the early sixties when I must have just started registering events as a small kid. It was altogether a different place to live in. The city used to be abuzz with the sirens of the mills and ever ringing bells of rickshaws. Smoke emitting chimneys were a regular sight. Water sprinkling tankers, built on old 'Ford' truck chassis, settled the floating clouds of dust as traffic moved past. At times, in the evenings you would also find a bhisti – man carrying water in his goat-skin bag, splashing water along the road-sides laden with dust. Roadside vendors of all shades like the *chaatwala, makkuwala, kulfiwala* and *pattiwala* used to frequent the lanes and bye lanes of the city during day time. In the evenings, it used to be the turn of *channa-jor-garamwala* and the hawkers of *eveningers*, who yelled the scandalous headlines of the daily evening tabloids that were published, just to hoodwink the gullible and trick them to buy rubbish.

Until the late fifties, the frontal footpath of UHM Hospital used to have a row of wooden shops (large '*gumtis*' type) collectively known as the 'Refugee Market', which eventually got shifted to the newly built Naveen Market in the early 1960's, when these shop owners were allotted permanent shops. This Naveen Market was quite small in size in comparison to the present day Naveen Market, and had 'Kundan's Shoes' as the last shop. It was extended much later.

Life as it used to be then, was much simpler with no exhibitionism, no hawkish appearances and show-off tendencies whatsoever, in total contrast to the present day vulgar displays. Things generally used by the middle class people were available for the asking and in plenty, as there were not many takers of items and services. More than anything else, people were conscious about their personal reputation and societal standing. Every small matter hinged around deep rooted moral values. Even business dealings used to be governed by such high moral standards that they developed into very personalized lifelong relationships. Short term immediate monetary gains had no value whatsoever in relation to everlasting personal bonds.

The city used to be full of rickshaws apart from *tongas* and a few *ekkas*. Of course, cars were there but negligent in numbers when compared to their numbers today. Scooters were yet to make their mark. Things like *tempos* and mini-buses were not heard of, as they were still to be conceived. City bus service was available but its frequency was abysmally low for a likely commuter to discard it as an option; and, I am told that until the early 1950's trams also used to adorn the city. So bicycles were the main mode of personal transport, whereas rickshaws used to be the main mode of public conveyance.

Cricket test matches used to be the main attraction and looked forward-to annual event because of which, the city could feature on the global map. A cricket test match in those days was the one undisputed event which used to get unchallenged publicity and the attention of one and all, as there was no other source of entertainment except for movies, which meant watching in closed door cinema halls. There was no TV, no VCR - so no black and white or blue film, no cables, no multimedia indoors and perhaps, no live shows (I cannot say for sure, since I was young then, to know) either. So a test match used to be a big gala affair like a function in the city, in which the entire city used to be drawn in, one way or the other. Everyone would start preparing together for it, months in advance. In a way, it used to be similar in spirit to a true *Nagar Utsav* of olden times stretching to a six days celebration.

In the absence of a TV, the only option was to either visit the stadium for watching the match live or remain contented being glued to the radio for the running commentary. The stadium would start getting official attention a few months in advance. Roads leading to the stadium would be repaired. Though there was hardly any hotel worth its name, the one which was there of whatever standing and repute, would get spruced up to accommodate the teams. Field and the pitch would be inspected and laid. The boundary walls of the stadium would be repaired and painted. The pavilion and the commentators' box would be given a face lift. And most importantly, the score boards would be given a thorough overhaul. In fact, these were the score boards which were the pride of the stadium and the town as well. These score boards were the only ones of their type in the world, which displayed each minute detail of the match – "Who was playing, who was bowling, how many balls had been bowled; and the detailed statistics of runs, wickets, maiden overs registered, and even in whose hands the ball was there from time to time". Tracking the ball right from the time the game started until the end of the day's sessions was the unique feature of the boards, literally. 'You ask for it and you have it'. You did not need to listen to the commentary if you were watching these score boards. In fact, most of the time we used to follow the game through these score boards even while watching the match inside the stadium from the various galleries, as it was quite difficult to make out, where the ball was with the naked eyes. Perhaps, at times, the commentators also used to fall back on these score boards for help, when in doubt. Truly versatile, these score boards were all mechanized and manually operated, designed by the local talent and cricket enthusiasts, as electronics and chip culture had not yet arrived.

In those days, cricket used to be the game of princes and the Lords. Though concepts like betting and match fixing still awaited debut, some of the haughty players from the princely states even in those days, were frequently seen violating the self-disciplinary regimen of the game. They were more famous for their royal lifestyle and eccentricities, rather than their playing skills. They were known to get up late in the afternoons on rest days, would never go for net practice with the other team mates and often indulged in late night parties. Perhaps, such violations of game discipline helped them maintain their distinct boorish identities from the other team mates, in being branded with the elite class tag and worshipped like heroes!

Of course, some of the commentators also, like these self-styled egoistic heroes, were famous for their garish appearances rather than their commentary. On some days, they would get 'high' in the morning and therefore, could hardly speak anything coherently and relevant to the live proceedings of the game.

It was indeed a treat to watch the excitement building up to a feverish pitch one rarely got to see otherwise, when the match dates drew nearer. Our house would convert into a sort of a *Chavani* (Cantonment), with relatives and acquaintances descending on our house from places like Lucknow, Allahabad and even from such far off places like Agra. The big hall of our house on the terrace would get converted into a dormitory, with each guest getting one cot and one shelf of a cupboard allotted for exclusive use. At last, when the D-day did arrive, everyone would get up very early in the morning to get ready. Ladies of the house too would get up very early in the morning, around 3.30 to 4.00 a.m. to prepare breakfast and pack lunch packets for everyone. The family would start from the house for the stadium early in the morning by 6.00 to 6.30 a.m. equipped with all the necessary paraphernalia and tools - a water bottle, a towel, a lunch packet, crunchy pop-ins to munch in between, sun visor or a cap and a few old newspapers to be spread over cemented benches in the stadium for sitting. Additional accessories among other things included oddities like balloons, crackers, rotten eggs, tomatoes and worn out *chappals*, which were meant for use as missiles in case of need; and, of course, a piece of mirror to reflect sunrays over the faces of players, for deriving sadistic pleasure, I suppose. In later years, as technology advanced, balloons were replaced by *Nirodhs*.

It was necessary to start early, as there used to be a lot of traffic restrictions imposed in and around the vicinity of the stadium and vehicles were not permitted anywhere near the stadium in a radius of about two kilometers. The culture of having red-blue lights or VIP passes for the vehicles had not yet pervaded. So normally people would prefer walking all the way to the stadium to reach around 7.30 a.m. It was a scene worth watching as the roads used to be swarmed by people moving in lots, as if the whole city had descended on the roads. And then, after reaching the stadium, one had to file in a long serpentine queue at the entrance that took no less than an hour and a half to reach its other end and disappear. Thus, one could be inside the stadium earliest by 9.00 a.m., but not before crossing all the hurdles.

Once you were inside the stadium, it used to be a mad scramble for a better seat for a vantage view of the play field, since the seats were un-numbered in most of the galleries. It used to be quite a free-for-all melee, jostling and pushing around, with everybody rushing and angling for better seats. Once one was through with the scuffle for a seat and occupied it majestically, it was time for the players' introduction to the Chief Guest, followed by the most exciting event of the first day - tossing of the coin to decide who would bat first. And one thing about this event, which always remained a hot topic of debate then, and still remains a mystery to me, is the ultimate identity of the possessor of the gold coin used in the toss. Was it the toss winning captain? The toss winning team? The umpires? Or, that a gold coin had not been used at all? There were all sorts of stories floating around and wild guesses being made, but no one had a definitive answer. No authority ever tried to clarify the issue either. Silence on the issue was pre-meditated and deliberate, perhaps not to spoil the fun and snatch the excitement associated with the game. As one of the bigwigs of the match organizing committee aptly remarked once that, it is better left a mystery.

During the period when test matches were held, there would be undeclared holidays in all the offices and all schools, colleges and institutions would remain closed for a week; and, everything would virtually come to a standstill.

At the end of each test match, whatever might have happened on the field and whatever might have been the result of the game, one thing was certain that at the close of the fifth day, everybody would have been drained of energy, completely exhausted and ended up with their faces and skin tanned brown.

Simple viewing pleasure in natural surroundings was what

constituted those golden days of life and entertainment! Alas! Things have now changed beyond recognition. The mills, which ruled the city once, are now totally defunct and in a dilapidated condition and have become like haunted places. Times have changed beyond compare. Nobody would believe now that I could hear the whistle as well as see the trains moving past the Medical College crossing at a crow flight's distance of about two kilometers from the verandah of our house in *Swarup Nagar*. There was absolutely no obstruction in between. One can hardly see anything beyond the gate of our house now, thanks to the concrete jungle!

Life has taken an entirely different turn, whether for better or worse, I do not know. At times I wonder whether it is the same place where I was born and brought up and learnt the first few lessons of my life! Perhaps, I have become an outsider in my own house and probably this is the way life moves on. I often brood on the pain and pressure that must have been felt by the old-timers of the city in the 1930's and forties due to invasion by outside families like ours, as we are feeling today due to the onslaught by the nouveau riche culture, typified by a pan-masala box in one hand and a 'mobile' in the other.

The old has to give way to the new, and the present has to yield to the future to become the past; perhaps, that is the way it is destined to be! It is sheer wishful thinking that the city of Kanpur could ever be an exception!

• KNOWING YOU •

PAROMA SEN

She called me in the middle of a busy Wednesday evening, at a time when I least expected anyone's call. I was lounging about with my friends when the phone rang.

"Can you help me? I seem to have crashed the car, although it's not badly damaged, I think I'm still going to need a mechanic ASAP"... those were the first words that gushed out of her mouth over the phone that day. I'll never forget them because it was but the first time she had ever called me.

Not that I expected her to call me and not that she had in the last three and a half years I knew her.

Since I didn't have her number saved on my phone, the unknown digits shocked me because… well, I don't like not being prepared. I almost had the urge not to answer the call. But something prevailed and I did.

It's not like she needed urgent help or anything. She just needed someone's reaffirmation that the damage to the car was not a big deal.

She lived about four blocks away from me. As soon as she got home, I went over to assess her version of the damage. Well, to put it simply, it wasn't as negligible as a scratch but not as severe as a serious dent either.

Like all men, the urge to help a woman in distress came forth spontaneously. I promised to have someone pick up the car the next morning to take it to the nearest mechanic.

Little did I know that this was just the beginning...

****

She has a dog. She chose to adopt a squirming puppy from the wayside - a small moaning one that had strayed. I always thought dog lovers were people who liked dogs. But she seemed to take the concept to a whole new dimension. She not only loved them, she cared for them. Right from street dogs to abandoned purebreds and every sort found a place in her heart.

In fact, the area outside her house was always packed with an assortment of street dogs, gathered there waiting for the little treats she kept putting out for them.

The next morning, as I left for work I saw her walking her dog, the one she had adopted and called her own. She just glanced at me; I think she was preoccupied with something else. I anyway drove by with a quick smile. I hadn't forgotten that on reaching work, my priority lay in sending someone to get her car fixed first.

The day wore on; her car was taken, repaired and brought back. I got caught up in work, so did she, I reasoned. But her better manners prevailed, a quick text to thank me for my generosity landed in my inbox.

That's how it actually all began.

I've never had a girlfriend. Surprising for not just someone but anyone in the 21st century, I know. But, a traditional army upbringing in a family that always moved about and then a career in the army led me to remain single, in the real sense. I met a lot of girls on the way, that's for sure. But I was never around long enough for any liaison to catapult into a real relationship. To be honest, I'd never even kissed a girl.

When she sent her *"Thank You"* text explaining why she needed to thank me and whether there was anything she could do in turn to genuinely reciprocate, a chain reaction of sorts started. I replied assuring her that a lifetime of hot freshly made paranthas and a lifetime supply of chocolate cookies would do fine.

Well, it's safe to add here, as a Punjabi, these are my two favourite things. It's also safe to add that I have a crass sense of humour when it comes to general conversations. Yes, I'm witty but not wise. Well...

It could have ended at that, but it didn't. Right after work that very day, she came over with a foil wrapped package containing my order of fresh paranthas. That was in itself a great shock. Probably because in these past few years of knowing her, not once had she made an attempt to get to know anyone in our environment. She liked to stay to herself and was always involved in her own world and things. I found this amusing. I found her amusing. But I had to admit, the gesture in itself was sweet.

Now that the hand of friendship had been extended, it was a whole new ball game in itself. Women, I've always maintained, have their own complications. In our environment, men mingling with women wasn't exactly a done thing. As army personnel we are often trained to be cordial to the opposite sex without ever crossing the line. She being another fellow officer's wife made her a person one could regard without being called a friend, by protocol, by an unspoken law of sorts.

You see, in the army, things are very different. Life is bound by your relationship with your seniors, how you address them, how often you get along with them and the like. Their wives are just their better halves you learn to deal with as comrades on the way.

****

Her first call had come in the cold winter months. I was just about to take off on a three week long leave back to my hometown in the North, incidentally right about then.

A week later and a few days before I left for home we ended up having a candid text chat. You see, you cannot chat up another's wife here, strictly speaking. While in the metro life that may be a normal possibility, things are a lot more reserved in the army.

It was during this chat that she told me how deeply I reminded her of someone she knew and almost married a long time ago. Someone she referred to as her first love. He had died in a terror attack back in her hometown a few years ago putting an end to the life she could have had with him before it even began.

This was a girl I had known since a while, without really knowing her. As part of the same unit, I met her often enough at army functions and parties, but never spoke to her beyond the credible hello, how are you and related pleasantries.

I wondered about her that night. How could someone so young, married to my senior officer have so much pent up emotion inside her, a personal trauma, a grief, something that made her who she was in many ways. Come to think of it, I hardly saw her smile; or laugh with a shine in her eyes - a clear sign that in her heart, everything was not alright.

This small text chat episode suddenly made me pay more attention to her. Why? Simply because she seemed like a big looming question mark to me. I suddenly felt the need to unravel this mystery of a woman who went about her daily affairs as if nothing were wrong when in fact everything appeared so.

Modern day technology has found many ways of allowing us to stay in touch with everyone we know and even those we don't. A trip home did not end our chats, in fact it intensified them. We started talking about silly things, making fun of each other, cracking jokes about the people we knew in common and even those we didn't. I suddenly felt more comfortable talking to her, considering the fact that I've never really had lengthy talks of any kind with any woman whatsoever in the past.

It slowly became natural to speak, at least for an hour a day, every day. What did we talk about…well to be honest, nothing in particular? That's what made the typed conversations all the more difficult to fathom. Yet, we had lengthy ones.

****

Army life is about not getting attached. In a way it is about getting ready to move on when you are just settling down. My posting or in simpler civil terms, my transfer order to a new city had just come through right around this time.

Well, that didn't matter on a personal level. The thought of visiting a new place for new work made it all worthwhile. As soon as I returned from my three weeks off, it was time to pack and leave. A sense of nervousness filled me, as is common when you have to close one door to open the other.

As I got ready, mentally and physically to leave Kanpur, a place I had merely spent about a year in, I was filled with a sense of happiness yet a slight feeling of discomfort dogged it. That was probably because I had just started getting to know someone for the first time. But well, in all it didn't matter much.

April came by, winter ebbed away and my truck was packed to the brim, with my life, my belongings, and proof of everything that was once me in Kanpur. I saw the truck off and followed in my car. Goodbyes were never my favourite thing.

A new place obviously meant a new journey. And that in itself was a thrilling experience. A week into my new role, I slowly started settling down. I hadn't shared my new local number with everyone yet. I thought of her. Not because of anything. Just because I wondered what she was up to?

I also wondered whether it was right in the army-way-of-life to give her my new number. After a week of thinking and serious contemplation I decided to go for it. How it could harm anyone, I mused.

So there, that's how the next chapter of our association began. Our text chats continued for weeks onward. Sometimes we didn't speak for days. Sometimes we spoke every day, sometimes all through the day.

We spoke about the weather, army protocols, what she did at work, how she lived her life, a little about her past, my past, what she liked. It all came out in a joking, competitive humorous way. We were never ones to have serious conversations. Another thing I never knew about her. She had a great sense of humour, a big open heart and a mind of her own. You couldn't ever really understand her. But you could begin to see what was inside of her, even if unclearly.

Days turned into months.

My new role seemed to take on new challenges and it is during this time that I found a kind of solace in talking to her every time we did. She seemed to have a way to lighten the darkest moments and in a way, I did the same for her every now and then.

It was through these chats that we found a way to not really get closer, because as you can see, in the army that isn't really allowed. But, we found a way to create a platform of sorts that worked for us thereby allowing us to be friends of our own kind.

****

April turned to July and to me the month was special not only because it was my birth month, it was the month I had bought my first car. I bet you can never really understand the immense joy a man experiences in owning his very first sedan.

It was customary of me to go home to my parent's once every quarter. I had last visited home before leaving Kanpur for my new posting. I missed home but couldn't seem to find the right time to take leave to go back.

July churned on.

I got the news early on a Sunday morning. My senior officer and brother in arms had passed away in a terrible car accident. His wife, who was with him in the car, was in a critical condition.

Instead of planning my trip home, I planned one to Kanpur first. Was it with the aim of grieving my senior's sudden death; in a way, yes? But it was primarily to see her and see how she was doing.

I reached Kanpur in a haze. It is a long way off from the southern part of the country from where I had left. There she lay on a hospital bed, staring at the ceiling. Her bandages made her look even smaller than she was. Her face had paled and eyes sunken in. I didn't have the courage to go right up to her so I waited at the door, staring.

I participated in all the regimental functions that are undertaken when a fellow officer dies. She sat through them too. I didn't know if she'd loved him, theirs was an arranged marriage after all. But I did know that they looked good together.

I had to leave because staying would have been painful. Her husband and I had known each other for years. I didn't know if it would be right to keep chatting with my new found friend. On the other hand, what kind of a friend would I have been if I didn't?

****

She eventually moved back home to her parent's house somewhere south of Bombay. The frequency of our chats reduced. But we did keep in touch. Life it seemed had to move on and she eventually started working. We met often till the time I was posted in a town close to where she lived. As it usually happens, she chose to get married again and so did I – however, to each other. We got married about a year and half after her husband's demise. It seemed the most natural thing to do.

Things change, people change. Life you see is a narrative of change.

****

Today, she called me up again and I can guarantee it was a busy Wednesday evening just like the last time. But she had to...who else would she have called when she had a problem. That was the thing with her. She panicked at the drop of a hat.

This time it wasn't the car but a very normal modern day problem. Her ATM card had gotten blocked. You see, this girl, she was one of those liberal independent kinds. You couldn't hold her down; you couldn't order her around either. I had always told her to keep cash with her at all times and not to wait till the moment she ran out of money to withdraw more, but she was never one to listen.

I had just come back to Kanpur after shifting base four times in the last few years. My new tenure in Kanpur was to last for a year at least. Life had turned full circle for me. She is here in Kanpur too, with me. My story started in this city - the great old Manchester of the East, and I sincerely hope that it will lead us into many more years of companionship together and take us to all the new places we are yet to be in.

I mean, we hardly thought it natural to not talk for days during our chat conversations post her first husband's death. Our conversations never seemed to end. Frankly, there was so much more to know when it came to knowing her.

Getting to know you, it seems, is going to take a while. But at least, we have all the time in the world now!

• A BLISSFUL JOURNEY •

JAYKISHAN

As a young man I had ambitions like any other guy you may or may not have met. I couldn't decide if I wanted to teach or become a consultant. But for someone born into a *Zamindari* family and not having seen his 23rd birthday yet, these were strange professions to choose. I was clear about what I wanted from life. It would be great to write reports that no one might read, travel the country at somebody else's expense and still manage to make money out of consultancy. But minds are tricky; they wander a lot and tend to settle on things which may never happen - whether it's a job or the choice of a profession or wanting to marry the girl you love.

So this story begins when a job was offered to me at the Administrative Staff College of India for what was then a princely sum of Rs. 1250 per month. Rs. 1250 per month to put it in the right perspective was more than what two engineers together would earn in a month as graduate trainees in that era. But alas! The story seemed to end even before it began. I had turned down the offer. The principal of the college was shocked at the attitude of this upstart of a young man who just didn't know what he was doing. My mentor tried bribing me by offering sops and a promise of a promotion which wasn't in his power to make. While it is quite fashionable these days to turn down fancy jobs it was unheard of in those days. The sordid saga ended when this young man did decide that home beckons and may be it was the desire of Mom's roti and dal or the lure of a comfortable home. Young *bania* boys were sent to earth to employ others and not be employed, said the Vedas; I seemed to justify my actions to myself!

And that is how I ended up in this little town which would later on become my home for the next 30 years.

I often wonder and reflect on what would have become of me had I taken up that offer. Perhaps I would have retired as the Director of IIM Timbuktoo, or closer home at *Jhumri Talayya*. *Jhumri Talayya*, by the way is a real town in Bihar, made most famous by "*Aap ki farmaaish*" on *Vividh Bharti*. Its claim to fame was the letter writing skills of its citizens who were proactive in sending song requests to All India Radio that they made themselves nationally renowned. By the way, to put the matter straight, that is not where I settled down. In case you might get any fresh ideas, I have never been to Timbuktoo either and except for having looked up the damn place in an atlas once to prepare for a school GK quiz, I would never have believed that such a city could even exist. Yes! Those days you still had what is called an atlas where you could look up names and places, turn the pages, try reading the cities off the bindings and still make a rainy day game out of that.

Coming back to my own little story, I came to what was then a quaint little town. I did not know a soul and was pretty sure I wouldn't last for long. But I've never been able to figure out the meaning of the word long. How long is long? One day, for some, is a lifetime for others. The drudgery of setting up a new business venture through the vagaries of bureaucracy was taking its toll. At the same time, I was wondering what the girl I loved and still do was getting upto. It's been 35 years and I haven't forgotten her one bit. The dimpled smile on her face, the hourglass figure and the sultry eyes all come to me in a flash. Where is she? What is she doing? Did she get married?

Does she have kids and will she remember me? But like I said; the mind wanders too much, and more often at the wrong times in all the wrong places.

If life were so simple there would be no need for God. He does make sure that you keep recalling him lest you forget your daily *pooja* and *daan patra*. So my elusive search for Meera was soon forgotten. Out of sight is out of mind. That by the way is the best way to control the mind. What you don't see won't hurt you.

I have felt sometimes that life is like a PG movie. Watch it under parental guidance and you will be safe. If you get caught without the cover you get thrown out. It is a lesson I learnt the hard way and do not regret till date. So it was a girl of my parent's choice. Let us call the effervescent looking one, Pyaari for the *pyaar* that she gives me, and the dusky looks which would beat Meera hollow any day. Now don't get me wrong. I loved Meera and I thought I couldn't live without her, but here was Pyaari sitting right across me in a blue nylon sari, which draped her so well and looking so longingly at me that I thought I instantly fell in love with her . Now Mills and Boon says it is just utterly impossible to fall in love twice, but if you've been watching enough Hindi movies of the older times you would do well to know that it was quite a common practice in our times really to fall in love twice, and as many times as you wished as long as nobody else learnt about it.

Well the *saat pheraas* were performed with Pyaari. With great fun and much fan fare. The nuptials of the eldest son of the eldest was too great an event in the family to miss. I never knew I had so many relatives who would actually travel from far and wide to meet young Pyaari and welcome her with warmth. It was great to be married you know, in a sort of a nice traditional ritualistic way. You know, what

I mean. After all, it doesn't happen every other day, does it? And, it's like a once in a life time event-to *get married and stay married, stupid!*

And so a great journey began with Pyaari. If I were to recount the best moments spent with her, then of course it surely had to be the holiday in the Andamans. That was when we were both trying to get over the seven year itch. Each evening we would sit in the hotel lounge and watch five young couples getting drunk to glory and then have the most rollicking time ever. That is the first time I saw one young woman drink half a bottle of black rum over one fun-filled night. But the twist in the tale was when none of them believed we were married for seven years. Well may be it was a compliment to Pyaari or may be to my standing as a lover. It worked like magic for us and then followed another blissful seven years, before we decided that another beach is just the place to rejuvenate ourselves. Where else but Mauritius. Those days Mauritius was the new flavor of the season. This trip has more memories than I can hold down. Not because they are too long but because fifty shades of grey would become green with envy!

The kids came of course. But do remember what I said about PG movies also holds good for PG accommodation. So while the kids grew up at home we travelled all across the world and wondering if this would ever end. Amidst all the dos and don'ts from uncles and aunties and those who knew more than most, we set upon our trip to Europe. Back packing so to speak. Italy is full of thieves they warned us and so we were strapped heavily to the teeth in a manner which would do a modern day terrorist proud. Rome changed our lives. Pick up a map at the hotel reception and walk the European cities to get a flavor of the country, they had said. Having seen the

Coliseum, we headed onwards when soon I had an eerie feeling. The road seemed to be too quiet to be good. How true, as two Vespas came zipping down the narrow cobbled alley, which in normal circumstances, I would have been comfortable with in Chandni Chowk. The argument we had in the hotel room came back to me with a jolt.

"What shall I wear today? " Pyaari asked.

"Wear the short skirt and tight top that we just bought at Marks and Spencer last week, though you did say you wanted to save it for some place warmer and less India friendly", I replied.

"No I can't wear that during the day; I feel awkward" Pyaari replied.

I had won that argument and was now dreading these loafers who took no time to set us up. The lane was so narrow that you could hardly see the sky. With tall rundown buildings on both sides, clothes hanging out to dry and two Vespas chasing us, I was terrified. Pyaari gripped my hand hard and held on to me for dear life and for the first time in my life I understood the meaning of fear. May be it was our prayers in the land of the Vatican or sheer providence as I heard the loud noise of a police siren. Relief struck. Pyaari never left my hand again and I never saw the sight of that skirt again.

The party scene in town was fantastic as long as it lasted. A city without a working disco, meant piling on to the drawing rooms of unit family homes and creating the kind of havoc that hurricane Katrina would be proud of. My choice of friends was as varied as chicken in a poultry farm!

"What are we going to do for our silver anniversary darling?", asked Pyaari quite out of the blue really.

It took me by surprise not only because the question was sudden but also because I hadn't realized until then that we had spent 25 years in marital bliss. Now when women ask such questions they are meant to be statements of intent. You have to figure out what the intent is because she isn't expecting a straight answer to such a straight question anyway.

"Well Uh", said poor me.

"What do you mean, Uh? We will of course have to celebrate the anniversary; won't we?"

"Yes darling. I mean, of course, we will" I stumbled, still not having figured out what was expected of me. Was it a big party or a diamond necklace?

What happened at the party will be another story, my friends.

I did always think that once mom's dal-roti wears off, I would get bored of all the life this drab little town had to offer. It grew on me and my Pyaari. That is what Kanpur did to us folks. This is where I earned all my money. This is where my kids have grown up. This is where I would wish to be when I retire.

****

To be continued.

• CLOCK WORK •

MUKUL KHATTAR

A red river flows through the streets, sweet chantings of abuses are heard aloud, the brown leaves on trees struggle to breathe and the callous attitude of the people can make the living shudder. The period doesn't matter. It could be the past, the present or the future. Time doesn't exist here - some believe that the city is caught in a time warp. It is beyond hope and the only thing that can save it is action.

Ruled by the vicious evil called '*Kaalu*' for years - the city is a death hole. No one visits the city nor can anyone escape. Those who do manage to pass through the walls are scared to return in aid of the city. The army have their personnel assigned, tanks are on stand-by, striker planes hover in close proximity but none dare enter the walls of the city. The only law that prevails in the city is Murphy's law.

No one has seen Kaalu. He is all around. You can't see him but only sense his presence. Some mistake him to be God who is unleashing his anger. But where there is no hope, how can God exist?

The citizens are beyond recognition. There is nothing left to differentiate them - all look alike. Kaalu has emptied their minds and replaced the cavity with smog. Their hollow eyes express no emotions, just emptiness. The '*Pith*' has turned the tips of their tongues black with sharp sticky ends. They now are only capable of making unpleasant, disturbing sounds.

The Pith is kept in the safe custody of the *'Vulturians'*. It is believed that the pith has the radiance of the sun and the capability of shining brighter than any star in the galaxy. The circumference of the pith is surrounded by a liquid substance called *'Dhara'*.

When Kaalu came to the city, he infused a part of himself into the Dhara and allured the people to drink it. Every sip snatched away a piece of the people's memory. Each thread of memory became a source of energy for Kaalu. Now the dhara encompasses the souls of the citizens, leaving Kaalu invincible.

The core of the Pith keeps the liquid together like a golden stream. It can be said that the Pith is the cause and the preserver of the epidemic. But, at the same time, it can also be the antidote. It is just a matter of vision.

There is no question of an uprising. The spark of a protest fails to ignite in these hollow minds. Only something out of the ordinary can save the city. After all nothing can remain constant even in the void.

The patterns are changing and I, the Void, can sense something is about to stir. As the dry wind blows through the Jajmau area, once an elite area with bungalows facing the crystal clear water of the Ganges, I can hear the pages of *'Nashtar'* turn. The *'Nashtar'*, possibly the first Indian novel, holds secrets of universal languages. On the surface it's about an ill-starred love but deep down it reveals the secrets of ancient Cawnpore. Originally written in Persian, then translated to Urdu and then into English, most has been lost but there will be someone or something that will be able to decipher the clues and patterns that lie in the book.

The book lays by a window, covered with dust and cobwebs. It radiates a struggling glow, as if someone with a light source is trapped within the closed book. I feel a sudden gush of dry wind. The book opens, the pages flutter, the dust slides away, the cobwebs crumble up into small silky balls and vanish. The periphery of the book glows. There is a new kind of dust on the book. It shines like stars in the night sky but it gives out warm light like the sun on a clear summer morning.

Forming a small whirlpool around the book, it sucks in the golden dust, changes its direction and heads towards the *Katchery Cemetery*. The clouds are darker than usual. The golden dust glitters against the pitch black sky as it gently settles on a tombstone. Like any other tombstone in the cemetery, it is broken on the edges, blackened with the soot, rough stone textures blended with the cracks. It seems as if the golden dust is mustering courage to defy the law of gravity, as it crawls up the headstone like a file of hungry ants reaching for a savoury treat. The golden dust makes its way through the cracks till it reaches a toasted Golden Tickseed. It blankets itself around the dead flower and soon after, I am forced to look elsewhere.

Elgin mills, once the cause of a million smiles, now home to lost emotions, lays motionless within me for about 4000 days. Orphaned by the State it is now the breeding ground for the Vulturians. It is in these grounds that the seed of evil and political war was sown. I am looking for the new force when suddenly, hundreds of Vulturians emerge, like pop-corns in a microwave, from the sturdy grounds of the mills. I can now sense Kaalu's aura. The Vulturians can sense it too and they begin to shriek. As the shrieks amplify, the ground begins to shake, rusted metal chains unfurl from beneath the grounds. Like scared crabs, the chains unleash themselves on the necks of the Vulturians. As they tighten their hold on the creatures' necks, alchemy begins, the chains turn into gold and Vulturians begin to grow taller and stronger. The creatures are overwhelmed with the new found pride and power that they receive from the clutches of the golden chains. The pale skin of the Vulturians now have dark hair all over, their red beaks shaped like pompous trumpets have circular ends that rotate and cut like a chain saw. Their wings so strong that they could stir the wind in any direction they like.

It is not the Vulturians or Kaalu that have my attention. It is a pain within me, a new force that is trying to reach out to me, but where to look for it? In me everything is lost. I concentrate hard and then move inside the red bricked walls. Amidst all the rotting machinery, a small piece of equipment lies with different sized spokes and gears interlaced forming a circle. In the middle of the circle, inscribed in golden letters are the initials H.S.

The wind grew stronger at the cemetery. The golden dust infused life into the flowers. The yellow petals blossomed and, sensing some kind of purpose, shed and spread themselves on top of the tomb. And as they rested calmly on the cracks, the soot on the tomb turned into dust. The wind formed a small whirlpool again, sucking up the dust from the tomb, to reveal the engraved initials H.S.

It all happened simultaneously. It is no co-incidence that the initials were revealed at the same moment. It all seemed to be part of a bigger mechanism, may be a part of a clock that needs winding. A clock that can wake the walking dead. A clock that can move the city.

The wind leaves the cemetery and enters the gates of the mills. The Vulturians blow their trumpets to warn Kaalu and others of the wind. All the creatures come together, form a circle, and flap their wings. The rising wind is sucked in under the wings. It now lays motionless in the centre of the circle. Deep sounds of discomfort are heard, as if someone is struggling to breathe. This is the inner voice of Kaalu. The sky becomes black. The presence of Kaalu grows stronger. A gravitational pull so strong that even I feel a part of myself consumed by it. While the wind at large rose towards the black infinity, there was something that remained unnoticed by the guardians of the Pith. When the wind approached the gates of the mills it left behind some golden dust that blanketed a petal and entrapped within the petal was a whiff of air.

The golden dust released the petal and it swayed towards what now seems to be the centre of the black sky. Just half way through, the petal, changed its direction and entered the machinery room of the mill through the broken glass of a window. The petal now rested on the initials, H.S., inscribed in the centre of the equipment with gears. Below the initials is a pin-hole with a golden ring around it. The petal now opens up, unveiling the invisible whiff of air. The air travels into the pin-hole. Levers within it begin to thrust against a hole like a mortar and pistol. The air multiplies, it travels deeper, down into the hole. *'Click!'* And that's the first movement of a sprocket. Soon, the frequency of the clicks increases and sprockets begin to move clockwise. A light illuminates the scene from the head of the equipment. It reflects on a machine opposite it and it reflects the light back in a new angle. Soon the combinations and the angles of reflection light up the entire room. Bouncing off the various surfaces, the light now forms an Ashoka Chakra. From the centre of the Ashoka Chakra a wave of light moves vertically upwards. The wave of light hits the ceiling, spreads across, exits the broken window and lightens up the sky with an image.

The image attracts the hollow eyed. The pattern changes. I feel the other force stronger now. The walking dead walk in one direction towards the source of the image. Kaalu and the Vulturians feel fear for the first time. They feel tricked and deceived but they know that they are invincible till the time they have the Pith in their custody. It's not a victory for anyone, it is just a movement in the right direction. What H.S. stands for will remain a mystery. The image in the sky will remain a matter of perception. The only thing that matters is that they all stand together at the entrance of the mill.

'*Dong!*' A white light blinds me. I sense time and my death. The winding of the clock must have begun, but it will never bring back what has been lost. It will take forever for the clock to wind completely. I foresee a new beginning but I see a war that will continue for time to come.

• THE CAWNPORE OF YORE •

DEEPAK KHATTAR

Leaving old memories behind, my father chose to shift from the picturesque valley of Dehradun to establish his dry cleaning business at Kanpur in 1959.

Kanpur, then, was popularly known as the 'Manchester of the East'. Elgin Mills, TAFCO, City Power House, Victoria Mill, and MP Oil Mill popularly known as Dalda Mill etc. were landmarks and industrial enterprises, which defined the Kanpur of those days. The mere sight of the towering boiler chimneys blowing steam and bellowing black soot in the heart of the city, with railway tracks running through the main roads leading to these renowned mills represented the pulse and the industrial might of a city in action. However, it was a shock for me to come to this city – such a far cry from the natural splendor of the serene hills.

The house where we stayed first was located in one of the lanes of Gumti No. 5; Kunj Behar, to be precise. Back then, the streets of Gumti No.5 Market devoid of crowds, had a thoroughfare for reaching the Gurudwara across the railway crossing. We caught the school bus for St. Aloysius High School every morning. The bus traversed V.I.P Road and Mall Road to reach Kanpur Cantonment with ease - what a contrast when compared to the present day scenario, with so many vehicles plying on the road almost throughout the day. When the bus service closed down, I started sharing a rickshaw with two other friends. Rather than following the regular circuitous route which our bus used to take, the rickshaw ride through the by lanes of Bakarmandi, Chamanganj, and Bara Chauraha etc. made us reach our destination faster.

During one of those days when I was returning home from school, I observed that the roads were crowded with temporary shops which had sprung up on both sides of the road near GPO and Ursulla Hospital. Businesses were being run by post-partition refugees from Pakistan. A sizeable majority of them were well settled at the Navin Market, while the others were seen to have preferred places like Govind Nagar, Lal Bangla etc. Over the years, virtually all of them have prospered.

Within six months of our arrival at Kanpur, there was a tragedy in the family with the untimely demise of my father at the young age of 40. We changed our house for the second time within a short span and shifted to Shyam Sunder Building, Karachi Khana. I became friendly with a few kids of my age, residing in the adjoining flats and started playing cricket with them in front of the building. Elders complaining of noise made us later shift the venue of playing to the nearby Phool Bagh grounds. I can't forget my eleventh birthday when a new bat gifted to me by my uncle, was snatched away while I was returning home after a game. I desperately ran after the young boy but to no avail, as he had hoodwinked me in the lanes of Ram Narain Bazaar and disappeared. I reached home disappointed, in tears, but my mother comforted me and made good my loss by buying me a new bat.

After a year or so, we shifted to yet another new house in Nawab Saahab Haata, Patkapur, which though located in a congested area, was in close proximity to the venue of our family business, managed by my mother and my paternal cousin (Bua's son). The muddy access lanes and the house with Indian toilet seats and no sewer lines was a sickly sight. We had to compromise for a year or so, until we got a decent affordable accommodation. I still recall an incident when I got slapped in the lane by a youth whose foot I happened to trample with the front tyre of my bicycle, while I was riding at break neck speed within the lane. We also regularly witnessed the religious procession undertaken by the Shias during the Moharram festival when they beat their chest with chains. I vividly remember that scene as any other curious kid would have. I had seen nothing like that before and would often wonder as to why one would hurt oneself (even in penance) in the name of religion. I started understanding the relevance of such rituals only much later as I grew up.

We later shifted to a house in Kidwai Nagar in a new colony developing in the South of Kanpur. Much was expected of this colony in 'N' Block but nothing seemed to have changed for years. It is only now that the place is coming up but still has a long way to go as far as development is concerned. Buying a bus ticket for 25 paise to travel from Mall Road to Kidwai Nagar Main crossing and then paying just another 25 paise to reach home on a rickshaw is something which has remained permanently etched in my memory.

Having studied the primary school classes in co-educational schools until class 3 and class 5 (in part) at Dehradun and for an year in Class 4 at Lucknow, it was quite a learning experience for me to get adjusted to life in an exclusive boy's school, when my mother got me admitted to the Lucknow based school, La Martinère, having failed to get admission in the local Methodist High School. Not only did I make new friends, but spending four years in the school as a hosteller gave me an insight into community living, away from the Kanpur home environment. Each visit from the school to Kanpur, either during the vacations or during the other holidays, was unique in terms of learning something new. The one which I remember the most is of my return trip to Kanpur with two outstation friends, who wanted to spend the weekend with us. As we got down at the bus station at Collectorganj (now Jhakarkhati), we hired a rickshaw and my friend from Jamshedpur asked me in Hindi whether it was true that Kanpur was infamous for the numerous abuses people unmindfully interlace their conversation with. Before I could answer the rickshaw puller remarked, "Kaun Ma.... Kehta hai!" To his utter amusement, we had a hearty laugh. Similar anecdotes carry on till date but their impact has mellowed down to a great extent.

Immediately after having graduated out of school, the Martinians were in touch for a while with their juniors in school. As a result of this bonding, the old boys and the college team used to frequently play friendly rugby matches in the wet slushy grounds of Brijendra Swaroop Park, Benajhabar Road during the monsoons, despite rugby being mostly unheard of in those days. As everyone got involved with their higher studies later, this phase of interaction too waned with the passage of time.

After four years in Lucknow and another three at Delhi University, I lost contact with all my school friends. It became a difficult task to come to terms with life at Kanpur and an equally tough task to make new friends. I joined Christ Church College for my post-graduation, but could not get used to the place, especially after getting to spend three years at Delhi University, North Campus. Time flew and one friend's introduction led to another and finally we were a bunch of 5-6 friends. Watching movies in the early seventies was the only source of entertainment and we had to pull strings to get tickets especially on weekends. Many of the halls like Nishat, Imperial and Sunder etc. have now closed down, yet fond memories of all of them remain afresh, despite the discomfort of them being non-air-conditioned. A bet that I had won against some friends culminated in getting to see a movie free; I cannot forget the details. Nana Rao Park swimming pool had just opened and I used to boast of my swimming skills at Lucknow to my friends. The six of us went there for a swim and they challenged me to jump from the topmost diving point. Gutsy as I was, I took the challenge and accepted the movie bet. I froze with fear on seeing the pool from the top. With my heart in my mouth, I jumped straight down with the water splashing all over. I had gone down in the pool of water, nowhere to be seen. I was greeted by a huge round of applause the moment I emerged out of the water. The bet had been won and the movie that we watched was at Novelty - Meston Road, Moolganj. But I did not disclose to them that I had missed most of the dialogues of the movie, as the jump had taken a heavy toll on my ears.

After 1975, life moved on with increasing responsibilities associated with family life, children and business and I became oblivious of what was going on in the city. Kanpur continued to deteriorate in all aspects - electricity cuts, water scarcity, filth and garbage on road sides with increased use of polythene. Gone were the good old days of the main roads being watered with water tankers, and the lanes with water stored in 'Mashals' and sprinkled by Bhistis.

Sophisticated malls have mushroomed to cater to one and all, but Kanpur as a city has gone from bad to worse as far as civic amenities are concerned. My 54 years' tryst with Kanpur encompasses all these and much more!

The Cawnpore of yore as a place in history had a rich heritage under the British. It's time its glory was restored!

• THE STORY OF 'THE STORY-TELLER' •

RISHABH PATEL

Tring- Tring-Tring -Tring

(Sorry! The number you have dialled is busy, please try again later.)

Tring- Tring-Tring -Tring

(Sorry! The number you have dialled is not accepting any calls at the moment, please try again later, thank you.)

I threw away my cell in anger. Ten minutes later, my cell phone started blinking, the ring tone blaring - Crazy Frog. A few seconds later, I picked up the call.

"Sorry! Dev, really very sorry" she apologized. "I could not take your call as I was busy discussing my higher studies with my dad. Why did you call - anything urgent?" she rambled on in a single breath without letting me respond.

"That's fine, Anu. So what have you decided?" I asked her.

"Umm… We i.e. my dad and I have concluded that I should take admission in the B.Com course in a college affiliated to Delhi University". "That's good", I exclaimed with joy.

Then, she asked me the purpose of my phone call impishly.

After a pause of five seconds, I started again.

"Hey Anu, can you arrange accommodation for me?"

"Is there any problem, Dev?" she asked in a low voice.

"Hmm…yes, there is a problem."

"What?"

"Will you let me know whether you can help me in searching for accommodation?"

"Yeah! Why not? After all, you are my best friend. Why not stay at our place?"

"I will talk to my Dad about it."

"OK! Chal, bye; take care, talk to you later."

"Bye! Take care."

It was the last call that I took that night in Kanpur from my favorite ten digit number.

****

It was 3 a.m. and everyone except me was fast asleep. I had not slept the whole night. I switched off my cellphone and spent the whole night crouching at the corner of the bed pensively.

After a while, I stood up, took out a notepad and starting writing:

Dear Mom,

    Sorry! I cannot live in this house any more. No one cares for my feelings, my wishes and my dreams. I am going to leave this city as soon as possible, but one day I will come back, if you wish. Do not ever try to look for me.

Your loving son

Dev

Putting down the notepad on the dining table, I silently tiptoed out of the house all alone with my bag and wallet. I took the ticket for the very first train leaving Kanpur Central for New Delhi.

It was afternoon when I reached New Delhi station. I messaged Anu with my new number asking her about the accommodation. She called back.

"Hey; hi!, I exclaimed.

"Hey! guess what". She replied in an excited tone.

"What?"

"Dad, agreed, but …?"

"But what?"

"Actually, he wants to decide about your staying at our place only after meeting with you in person. He wants it to be informal."

"OK. That's alright."

"Hey! Where are you calling from? Are you at the New Delhi station? I can hear the PA announcements being made."

"Aye! I am here, at the New Delhi station."

"Oh! God, you are a real jerk; wait, I am coming as soon as possible."

"OK!" I said

I cut the call, and started looking for the waiting room. I could locate one without too much problem. I settled down in the waiting room and started checking the admission cut-off marks lists of Delhi University. The crazy frog started ringing again after about half an hour. I picked up the call.

'Hey!'

"Where are you?" she inquired.

"I am in the waiting room."

"Wait, I am coming there."

"Hey Dev!"

I could immediately make out that it was her voice - sweet, innocent and cheerful. I turned back to have a glimpse of her.

Having become best friends on a social networking site and coming face to face for the first time, I fumbled sheepishly. When she hugged me, I was a wee bit taken aback. Though it seemed quite natural to her, I felt terribly uncomfortable.

I simply gazed at her, awestruck. She was a real starry-eyed beauty, simply dressed with no make-up; no sign of attitude - a perfect girl. After a few moments, she chuckled.

"So, Mr. Devashish Shukla, are you ready for the interview? "

"Yes!" Miss Anushka Bhadoriya.

"So, shall we leave?"

"Yes! Why not?"

She steered the way to the car parking, and we left for her house. The drive to her house took 25 minutes. Her house looked imposing – no less than a palatial mansion. After a formal introduction, the first not so formal interview of my life (and that too- by the father of my best friend), was about to commence. Those were the most excruciating moments of my life - moments on which my future was likely to depend. Everyone else had quietly left the hall, except

Uncle and me.

Uncle – "What is your name?"

Me – "Devashish Shukla."

Uncle – "Where are you from?"

Me – "Kanpur, Sir."

Uncle – "What is your father's business? And why do you want to study here?"

Me – "Sir, I have been brought up by my grandparents, and I do not want to trouble them any more at this stage of their life. The least that I wish to do is stop being a burden on them. I can take up a part time job here to fend for myself while studying."

Uncle – "Oh! I am sorry son; I misjudged you. You seem to be a mature person. My best wishes to you for a bright future. Good luck. The house is all yours; you can live here but on one condition…"

Uncle – "Do not call me Sir."

Me – "Thank you, Sir."

The interview was over.

As soon as Uncle left the hall, Anu asked me to go to her room.

I followed her like a child.

She – "Hey, what is this?"

Me – "What?"

She – "Why did you lie to my father?"

"Lie"? - I asked her, astonished.

"Yes, Mr. Shukla, a lie! I distinctly remember you telling me earlier that your father is a reputed lawyer of the Kanpur Bar Association and your mother, a social worker. Why did you then hide the facts about your parents?"

"Yes, but do recap the dialogue I had with your father. I never said that I do not have parents. I only said that I was brought up by my grandparents and that is true", I replied confidently.

"The way you said it, meant that you do not have parents." She raised her eyebrows in a questioning manner.

I felt like an accused who has murdered someone in front of a cop. I felt trapped and gathered my confidence, enough to reveal the truth.

"I did not tell your father about my parents because I had run away from home. In fact, I had left behind for them a letter asking them not to search for me", I muttered.

"What? You ran away from your house? You are really disgraceful. I am disappointed in you", she said.

"Don't be angry Yaar; I had my own reasons", I replied.

"I want to know the reasons", she said in an angry tone without looking at me.

"OK, if you want to know, I will tell you", I retorted back.

"Hey! Anu! Can we please sit on the bed; my legs are aching?" I pleaded.

Visibly amused, she said, "Yes! We can."

It was apt for me to reveal the truth. I began at the start.

That fateful day when my mother and I were preparing to leave Kanpur for admission in Delhi University, neither of us knew what was in store for us. It was like any other routine day. My father had come back from his office on time. He however came directly to my room that day, which to my mind then, was quite an unusual thing to happen. He sat by my side on the bed and remained silent for a while; but all of a sudden, started questioning me about the scope of journalism and mass communication as a career option.

"What?" I looked at him in an astonished manner.

"Yes son, tell me the scope of journalism and mass communication - the course that you have selected", he asked me pointedly.

I explained to him in detail everything I knew about journalism and mass communication. My mother and sister too came into the room and sat silently without interrupting us.

When I stopped, there was again the same heart breaking silence, which I hated the most. That silence was killing me.

Suddenly my dad started again, "How will you live in such a big city? What about your food?" He kept on asking me many more probing questions, uninterruptedly.

I chose not to answer him because I didn't have answers to several of the questions posed by him. I didn't want to have an argument with him, because I knew it was futile to have one. So I preferred to keep quiet, but I knew that my silence was going against my interest.

He got up and said, "Neither are you going to Delhi nor taking this course for your higher studies. Prepare for either IIT or CAT - the choice is yours".

Adamant that he was, he didn't listen to me. I requested him to consider my choice of subjects but every attempt of mine failed to convince him. They left the room. No one in the family could dare to oppose him. I was left alone in the room, with no support from anyone. I felt like a small child whose favorite toy had been crushed.

I wanted to cry as loudly as possible but my voice failed me. I buried my head in my lap. Although I wanted to scream, I could not. I sat there emotionless, helpless and without any hope.

I spent the whole night sitting at the corner of the bed brooding in the same crouched posture and remained glued to my room almost for the entire day. In the evening, as if with a sudden rush of adrenaline, I decided to move ahead; I made up my mind not to quit, but to break my ties with everyone. I did not wish to live in a place where one's emotions, dreams, feelings, and thoughts were not valued.

When I had completed my narrative, I noticed that Anu's eyes had turned moist; she was crying silently.

"What happened?" I asked her, as I wiped her tears.

She remained quiet for a while and then hugged me. I also hugged her in affirmation, though briefly.

She whispered cautiously; "Sorry! Dev, really sorry; I did not have any idea that you were going through so much mental turmoil".

"It is OK."

****

"Ye leejiye, Sir; you are at your destination, "said the cab driver.

I handed him a thousand-rupee note and asked him to keep the change.

"No Sir, you are one of the best story tellers I have ever come across. I have become your fan. How can I accept money from you? Thanks for narrating such a nice story", said the taxi driver and drove away.

I was standing at the gate of my ancestral house in Kanpur - my city, after a gap of 6 years, mustering all the courage to go inside and face my kith and kin. Yes! I am afraid; I am afraid at the kind of treatment that awaits me. What will they say? How will they react?

Things have not changed much except that the 16 year old boy is a 22 year old youngster – a bestselling author of the country, a wild life photographer and a story teller – all rolled into one.

One might achieve anything and everything following a fit of rage, but not when one is afraid. My mind goes back to the lingering question, again and again: What if I had not shown courage to leave home that day?

• A CHILDHOOD TRAPPED •

MONIKA PANT

I vividly remember that house where I used to spend my childhood holidays - the old, dilapidated tenement flat in Kanpur, where my grandparents lived. It haunts me still. The past visits me often as though offering me with a kaleidoscopic view of my life experienced so far. Disjointed images, some happy, some sad, some furious with the way the world was, and some when I was at peace within – all form these jumbled up patterns; and align themselves perfectly like coloured pieces of glass to form a magnificent spectrum.

It was an oft visited house, dearer than the home I lived in at Lucknow. This was a place of dreams, of childhood captured in snatches of innocent laughter. I have lived in much larger bungalows since then, in spacious duplex houses, in sprawling mansions and modern flats; but, the flavour of that ground floor house in *Souterganj* is permanently etched in my mind; and, my heart fills with a unique exuberance when I think of the days spent there.

The cracked coloured glass in the panes of the door that led to a tiny outer courtyard was something only ground floor residents had. The other floors had narrow balconies that ran along the façade of the building, little balconies where potted plants were kept and a child or an old lady could be seen looking out at the people on the road ambling along; for life genuinely ambled along, way back in the 1970's.

Every couple of months in the 1970's, I would look forward to going there with my parents - sometimes by bus, at other times by train in the second class compartment that most middle class people travelled in. It was only a two hour journey that added to the charm.

My grandparents' abode had the luxury of an inner as well as an outer courtyard; and, I would get up early in the morning to pick little mauve periwinkles growing there, put them in a small basket with a few blood red hibiscus flowers and give them to my granny for her daily morning puja. I remember the crisp air, the few cyclists, milk vendors and newspaper boys on the street I could see, as I balanced myself on the jutting-out bricks of the paved area of the courtyard attempting to stretch out for a particularly glistening new leaf that had sprung up during the night and was hanging tantalisingly, just out of my reach, on the branch of the big Ashok tree in the corner. I remember sitting at the huge oval dining table waiting for my milk and biscuits and later for those round fluffy 'luchis' - little thin roundels of wheat bread, fried to a golden colour with fat slices of brown, juicy brinjals. It used to be like icing on a cake when the *luchis* were served with tangy tomato chutney.

I remember the gaping hole on the stone slab over the big sewer that flowed past the house, which we, as children were cautioned about, but found fascinating as we espied our toffee wrappers ride the swirling waters beneath our feet. The numerous wooden letter boxes with house numbers written in black paint on them; and, the excitement of finding a letter in it is a forgotten relic, as emails have come to rule our lives and no one writes letters now. The faint smell of wet washing on the clothesline, mildewed walls and incense sticks mingled with Indian spices created a heady fragrance that still clings to my senses.

Later, of course, when I was older and in love, I used to sit in the courtyard with his love letter between the pages of my novel, reading, re-reading it and staring into the patch of sky; with the strains of a popular love song wafting across to me from a loudspeaker at some unknown function in the vicinity. A song of the late 1970's, perhaps which would be remembered by all those who belong to that time; "*O Saathi Re, Tere Bina Bhi Kya Jeena…*" had captured my imagination then; and I would hum along hoping that my words would reach the ears of my beloved (there being no such thing as a mobile phone in those days).

The Durga Puja celebrations by some known families in the city, the weekly visit to Naveen Market, the Elgin Mill and its lovely, brightly coloured towels and bed sheets, the *Motijheel* and the wonderful zoo with animals in their natural surroundings were some other things that will remain etched in my memory. The dreams of my childhood and youth have remained trapped in the cracks of the chequered black and white floor on which I spent the hot afternoons playing 'snakes and ladders' in poorly sunlit rooms. The radio belting out melodious numbers in Mohammed Rafi's velvety voice and the uproar while playing cards right through the vacation days echo in my ear whenever I think of those idle, languorous days melting into fun-filled evenings. The thrills of getting dressed to go for a night show in the neighbourhood theatre and the mere sight of melting ice cream cone trickling down sticky fingers are unparalleled and cannot compare to the ephemeral joys of today.

A house or a dreamland, a childhood haven or a refuge for my bruised heart – it was my grandfather's residence that used to be the ultimate destination and he, my hero. Later, when he lay on his deathbed, I had gone to visit him there. An emaciated form, quite a different one from the sprightly figure he used to make earlier on his morning walks on the streets of Kanpur, he encapsulated the essence of my childhood home. I sat by him as the clouds gathered overhead; we both recounted some incidents from the past, many, many unspoken remembrances crowding around the two of us. He died that year, and with him died my association with the house that had breathed with me and hidden my secrets like a dear friend.

Now, if I go there, there are new tenants in the house, and the coloured glass panes are no more. The Ashok tree has gone too and along with it, my sighs that were entangled in its boughs. Indelible memories of a bygone era are frozen in my mind - akin to chunks of shiny bright glass embedded in concrete.

• IRONY OF LIFE •

FATIMA MAHMOOD

That breezy morning brought in a whiff of cheer to delight me. The academic results had been declared! I had done very well in the just concluded MBA final examination! A sense of accomplishment dawned over me with the completion of my studies. I felt happy that I would be on my own feet and I had to no longer rely either on my uncle's money or my scholarships. I was lost in thought, when suddenly Ayush, a friend of mine, called up and started reeling out the details of the impending convocation ceremony in an excited monologue.

Despite Ayush's call, I could not pull myself out of the web of random thoughts. A mixed feeling clutched at me. While on the one hand, it had indeed been a very proud and satisfying moment for me for having scored excellent marks; but on the other hand, realizing that it was the last day at college, the very thought of leaving college was very depressing. Even more disturbing to find out, which was akin to rubbing salt over my wounds, was my favourite professor Mr. Tripathi's retirement.

The turning point in my life seemed to be just round the corner. I cheered myself by focussing on Mr. Tripathi, and attempting to dispel the turbulence in my mind.

Mr. Tripathi served our prestigious college with distinction for 34 long years. He had a distinct ideology of his own and a mellowed personality, ripened with age. Dark complexioned, with a diamond-shaped face, he donned a French beard apparently to mask the scars left from chicken pox at a young age. His attire was quite unlike the other professors and very much at ease in his kurta pyjamas, which he not only loved wearing but also attributed to his loving wife by acknowledging; "My wife loves me in this attire". It was at the instance of his wife that he opted for the VRS, we were given to understand. He seemed really happy at the decision and had no regrets at all.

Mrs. Tripathi was another gem of a person, like her husband. Extremely good at heart, she was the humblest lady I have ever met. Very jovial by nature, she was adept at cooking. Sick and tired of the nauseating food served at the mess, I used to visit Mrs. Tripathi often. Her hospitality notwithstanding, she used to treat me to very tasty dishes. Mr. Tripathi too displayed an interest in cooking, which was evident from the manner in which he used to assist his wife. Mrs. Tripathi's alerting her husband lovingly to taste the dish to check the salt content prior to serving often indicated the rapport they enjoyed while cooking together. That impressed me immensely.

When it came to food, my thoughts strayed to the true flavour of my own city – Kanpur. Food of all varieties are available at every nook and corner of the city, be it South Indian, North Indian or even Chinese – one can have it all.

However, I started wondering whether I would be lucky enough to find a wife like Mrs. Tripathi, who to my mind was an incarnation of the Hindu Goddess, Annapurna – the Goddess, who feeds; in fact, every woman of Kanpur in a way, has the blessings of the Goddess.

While I was persistently absorbed in my thoughts, a man came and stood in front of me, smiling.

"How is it going son?" he asked.

He came well dressed in ebony black coloured Blackberry formals. Holding a bouquet of flowers in his hands, it was Mr. Tripathi; yes, it was for the first time that he had been seen in such an avatar.

"Sir! I'll miss you the most", I told Mr. Tripathi sadly – the person whom I idolised.

"So will I, Rajat; you are the best student any teacher can have", he said proudly.

"I'm not too sure whether I really deserve your praise, Sir, but, I'm quite upset with your decision of taking VRS; this college really needs you, Sir!" I replied.

"Ha-ha! I know; but more than the college, my wife needs me", he said.

"Whenever I used to get back home after a hectic day at the college, I found her reclining on the rocking chair, waiting for me; the food lying on the dining table, cold and uneaten; but, she never complained, Rajat. It's time for me to reciprocate. I want to spend the rest of my life with her".

I smiled and wondered as to how a man who had already spent 35 years of his life with his wife, was still in love with her, and so willing to be with her; may be because they were made only for each other, I mused. Their only son left without bothering about them, in tune with the current trend of sons abandoning their parents after coming of age. Mr. Tripathi was truly an inspiration to me, who not only imparted good knowledge of commerce but also made me realize the real worth of life.

"Sir, have a great retired life!" I wished him with reverence.

"I wish I could get this job, Sir. I hope I could delight you with some good news about my placement soon", I said.

"Why not? You have the skills and the qualifications and I'm sure, you will have many higher job opportunities in future. Rajat, just keep reminding yourself about how your mother brought you up singlehandedly and after her death, how your uncle refused support for your further studies. My son, you have reached where you are, on the strength of the scholarships that you have won on your own merit; so why the despair now? You shouldn't lose hope. If not this job, then let it be another job. Just never stay indolent."

Those were his finest words that always worked like magic: "Just never stay indolent".

"Keep yourself busy; no matter what the work be; just never stay idle"

I received a placement letter soon thereafter from a top automobile company with a package of 3.5 lakh rupees per annum. Mr. Tripathi invited me for dinner on hearing the news. I was swept off my feet on entering his house, by the enticing smell of Matar Pulao.

"Here cometh my son, stated Mr. Tripathi, boastingly. Muniya, please bring cool Rooh Afza for Rajat", he instructed his wife.

The manner in which the lady of the house was lovingly addressed charmed me. Mrs. Tripathi once told me that their love story gained strength, when they fortunately met munching 'paani ke bataashe' (water balls) at Swaroop Nagar. The hawker was humming the popular 1966 Hindi film song sung by the late Manna Dey, "Chalat musafir moh liyo re pinjde wali muniya" while serving the bataashe.

Mr. Tripathi chose to call his wife 'Muniya since then, it seems – like the true Filmy-Indian-Couple of the sixties!

"I made a special pudina chutney for you, with a pinch of ambiya (raw mango) in it; hope you like it", Mrs. Tripathi said humbly.

"I will love every fibre of it", I grinned.

The couple settled to dine and Mrs. Tripathi served me first and then her husband, gently nudging, "Better eat properly" with her beaming smile. Another captivating quirk about the couple was that they used to eat on the same plate that always made Mrs. Tripathi oversee her husband's eating demeanour, because he was a messy eater quite unlike his organised teaching reputation.

After spending a memorable evening with the iconic couple, I bade goodbye to them. Mrs. Tripathi caressed my hair tenderly and Mr. Tripathi proudly repeated his favourite line:

"Rajat, you are the best student any teacher can ever have", with a glint in his eyes.

Time passed by as I got firmly entrenched in my work environment with a good natured boss in a decent job. My work, presentations etc. was well appreciated which kept me motivated too. I was well settled and got married to a colleague from my office, which to my mind was timely. Considering the miseries I had confronted in my childhood and remembering how my mother managed to buy one meal for the whole day, my life could not have been better; I was a blissful person at last. In the heart of my hearts, I sincerely gave every piece of credit to my mother and my most respected teacher Mr. Tripathi. His guidance and the lifelong learning from his mantra "Just never stay indolent" always put me on the right course. I never knew however that there was more in life to wade through.

Three years rolled by; I was having lunch on a sunny Sunday afternoon with my wife and son, when I received a call suddenly from my friend Ayush who told me that Mr. Tripathi's wife had died due to a heart attack two days earlier. The news shocked me; I was filled with grief. She was like a second mother to me. Ayush called me to inquire if I could accompany him to Mr. Tripathi's house for offering condolences.

"No! I have tasks to get done. I'll come later"; I refused him in a subdued tone.

My refusal was far from the truth; the truth was that I lacked the courage to confront Mr. Tripathi's agony. No one besides me knew how genuinely they both loved each other. What would he be doing that entire day? How would he face the jolt of such despair and solitude? I was afraid that he might attempt suicide in desperation.

Despite my wife's persistent efforts, she could not succeed in making me muster enough courage to meet Mr. Tripathi. I remained adamant. I went to my office to divert my mind. It was of no avail as Mrs Tripathi's death became my Achilles' heel. I was unable to do anything, so I decided to leave office early. While driving back home, I stopped at Gumti No. 5 to buy some broccoli my wife had asked me to bring. My eyes caught a forlorn person standing nearby. I focussed my stare on that face again, with deepened wrinkles and a bent back, but saw the same glint in his eyes. Yes! It was Mr. Tripathi standing just a few blocks away from me. I still couldn't gather enough courage to meet him. By then, he himself exclaimed,

"Rajat, my son; my Muniya left her Musafir to travel all alone".

The moment Mr. Tripathi uttered those words; I couldn't hold back my tears. I just didn't bother about the crowd around me; I cried my heart out. Mr. Tripathi gently patted my back, and asked me to walk with him. On the way, he told me that my wife had called him up and briefed him about my predicament and of my reticence to meet him. She had prevailed upon him to meet me, when I had been intentionally sent by her to the market on the pretext of buying broccoli.

"Your wife reminded me of Muniya; even she used to trick me this way, but always for a good cause", reminisced Mr. Tripathi.

"Sir, I'm sorry; I was not there for you in your difficult time, when I should have been there", I mumbled in repentance.

"It wasn't all that harsh Rajat; you should have seen her. It wasn't like she died; it was as if she had gone into a deep sound sleep, with her face at her divine best", Mr. Tripathi said, peering at Mrs. Tripathi's photograph kept in his wallet.

I was as quiet as the sea, which had turned silent after levelling out its heavy tides. We reached his home; he made black coffee for me and for himself. His house was pregnant with Mrs. Tripathi memories; I was unable to believe that she was gone.

"Her heart seems to have failed due to high cholesterol. She never took my repetitive warnings of the ill effects of oil seriously. She always came up with silly excuses to justify the use of excessive oil. She thought that's what made her cooking tasty. The adamant lady has abandoned me to eat all by myself, all alone", Mr. Tripathi said, by abruptly gulping the black coffee, as if he was gulping the sorrow amassed inside him. He then intentionally changed the topic.

"Anyway, how are you placed with respect to your job? It is great to learn that you got married and became a father recently." He inquired further about my life.

"Everything is fine, and yes, my son is almost 5 months old now", I said.

"That's great, convey my love to him. Rajat, can I ask you for a small favour? He asked hesitatingly.

"Why not? Please do not embarrass me; it is your right, Sir!" I intervened.

"My wife is gone forever and she is not going to come back. I get bored every day. I don't feel good staying back home indolent; I have nothing to do, except waiting for my death knell. I went to our college as well; they say I am too old to be a professor now. So I was wondering if you could arrange any kind of job for me in your office", he elaborated further.

Life is so mysterious, I mused. I started wondering about the irony of life - how a working man seems to have lost his bearings and a non-working man turned into a working professional. How my teacher's own ideology of "Never stay indolent" had fallen short of his beliefs when it came to himself. My mind became surcharged with anxiety and pity for Mr. Tripathi. Nothing worthwhile triggered my brain that could redeem this old man's plight and pain.

The only thing I could say was, "I'll speak to my boss."

"Thanks son, I wish I get this job, hopefully" stated Mr. Tripathi, expectantly.

I went straight to my boss's cabin the next day and narrated the entire episode to him.

"Rajat, I do understand his condition, but you are aware that he is 64 years old. What would he be able to do at this stage in life; probably, serving tea in the cabins or dusting the office windows and corridors? If he is willing to do such jobs then let me know; Yes, you can rest assured that I'll pay him a decent and appropriate salary because of your reference", my boss replied.

Startled at the reply given by my boss, I quipped, "Thanks for your consideration, Sir; however it's not needed" I left his cabin hurriedly, angry at my own helplessness.

I was driving back home when suddenly I saw a boy having an ice-cream with his grandfather at the Mall Road parking. Both seemed happy, chortling in joy. Within a flash, I rushed to Mr. Tripathi's house. He came out and inquired,

"What did your boss say?"

"You have a job to do"; I smiled and asked him to come along with me.

Mr. Tripathi happily sat in the car; I drove back home and asked him to come inside. Without a clue, the old man gazed at the house and asked,

"Is this your house Rajat?"

"No, it's your place of work and it's our house", I asserted.

Mr. Tripathi stayed quiet for a while; sharp that he was, he understood everything in a jiffy and rejected my proposal outright.

"I don't want this job; I don't want people to watch me with pitiful eyes as a hopeless aged person living at the mercy of others in their house; I want to earn and live. I want a job for myself on my own merit, so that..."

"There is a job for you, I interrupted in between. Not one but many jobs; your job is to assist me in taking the right path when I'm going wrong; your job is to keep this house alive with good morals just as you kept your house; your job is to nurture my son with good values and ethics in life, in exactly the same way as you guided me when I was with you; your job is to praise and criticize the food prepared by my wife just like you used to do with Mrs. Tripathi; And most significantly, your job is to be the most respectful and eldest person of our family. Now tell me whether you will accept me as your son?"

Mr. Tripathi's eyes brimmed in tears, and rolled down his wrinkled cheeks and he proudly stated:

"Rajat, you are the best son any father can have."

I couldn't contain myself and embraced him with all the love and reverence I had for him. And then holding both his hands, I pronounced:

"You have got the job, but I have earned a father."

Life can be rewarding too, for the persevering – it was a win-win situation, both for Mr. Tripathi – nay, my father and me.

• THE CITY OF LOVE, LIFE & PASSION •

BHAVIKA MATHUR

While packing my bags, I was in a dilemma of sorts about my life. I took a deep breath and started packing the scattered things lying around. I was a bit nervous, in fact, very nervous as I didn't know what to do next. I was however sure of one thing; that I had decided to run away from home to escape from my family, 'cruel' as far as I was concerned.

Well, "Hi!" Let me introduce you to the girl on the verge of preparing for the great escape, within moments after her parents fell asleep. It was none other than yours most truly. "Yes!" You've got me right. Sanchi, away from home, out into the world she barely knew.

I know, no one talks about one's parents so dismissively, but they were the type of people who ought not to be spared. They used to scold me every time without any reason especially when I went out with my friends. They tortured me if ever I was seen talking to a boy, even if he were to be my classmate. Even when I asked them to permit me to take admission in a reputed college of Management Studies located in another city, they refused flatly.

That was when I decided to leave my home and run away somewhere.

When my parents had gone to attend the marriage of a cousin, I decided to leave home once and for all. I knew I would be losing out on the job that I was doing then. I consoled myself that the job had at least provided me with the security and the money needed for my immediate survival.

I packed up my bags and was ready to leave Gujarat forever.

Before leaving, I left a letter for them which read:

"Good Bye! Mom and Dad; I'm leaving home for good because I'm fed up with both of you. Hope both of you will be happy. Never try to search for me".

Never ever felt truly yours,

Sanchi

I don't know how my parents would have reacted, but they never seriously tried searching for me, I learnt later.

Well, leaving my past behind, I went to the station. I had absolutely no clue where to go. As if I were in a trance, I bought a ticket to Kanpur and boarded a train which was about to leave for Kanpur.

The train reached Kanpur in the morning at 6 a.m. I got down on the platform with my bags and started moving towards the exit gate at a swift pace. I was a bit confused as I didn't know where to go, but continued moving ahead with the swarm of people exiting the platform. As I was inching forward, I felt someone following me. I looked back and saw a boy behind me. He was about to say something, but before he could, I increased my pace as if I were racing. Within a few minutes, the boy was in front of me with a smiling face, holding my purse in his hands. He handed it over to me and told that I had dropped it at the platform, explaining the reason for his frantic chase.

I felt embarrassed but thanked him profusely for helping me, imagining my plight at an unknown place without the money. As he was about to leave, (I thought he might be the right person who could help me in finding rooms on rent or a paying guest {PG} accommodation), I asked him hesitatingly to help me once more, if possible, in finding rooms on rent or with PG facility.

He told me that there were rooms available on rent at his home, where he lived with his family. He asked me to come over and see the place, if I felt comfortable in going along with him.

I thought for a while about the brief and pleasant experience I had had with him and decided to accompany him. We hired an auto to Shyam Nagar where his house was located. Meanwhile, he introduced himself as Karan Sharma. He was an IT Officer in a bank, who lived there with his mother, his elder brother and his wife. It hardly took less than half an hour for us to reach our destination.

His home was quite good; it was a nice place with greenery all around it. I greeted his mother, his brother and his wife. We went inside and he narrated the entire incident of our chance encounter to his mother. His mother agreed to keep me as a paying guest after listening to her son's story and asked him to show me the rooms.

The rooms were nice as well as neat and tidy. I liked them and so decided to stay there. I deposited the cash with them towards rental advance and headed into the room for settling down. His sister-in-law, Aditi helped me in my efforts.

They were very friendly and co-operative people, who helped me in each and every way possible.

Within a few weeks, Karan and I became very good friends. He showed me the markets nearby, the malls, and every other joint I needed to know. He used to help me whenever I had any difficulty.

We both liked each other's company and started spending time together. We used to meet daily on the terrace or at our favourite ice-cream parlour, discussing the events of the whole day, after he returned from his office. It became our daily routine which we looked forward to, eagerly. These meetings which we liked doing virtually every day together, blossomed into romance and a mutual liking for each other.

After a few weeks, I joined a company as an Event Planner and started getting busy with my work. I didn't even have the time to meet Karan in the evenings due to my hectic schedule. Although Karan didn't like it he never revealed it openly. On the contrary, he was quite supportive at all times.

My job presented me with the opportunity to make many new friends in my office and to spend time with them. Rohan was one of them. He was a guy with a very strong personality and great charm. He was rich, handsome and a well-mannered person. He was intelligent and used to handle every problem deftly.

We used to spend most of our time together, as we were a team and used to handle the same projects. We liked each other's company. As a consequence, I started maintaining distance from Karan. Although he felt bad and left out, he never confronted me about it.

As my intimacy with Rohan grew, one morning he acquired the courage to propose to me to marry him. I was so happy that I said "Yes" spontaneously and agreed to marry him. It was like a dream to me and found it hard to believe, because of the sudden spurt of happiness and excitement.

I wanted to share this incident with my best friend, Karan. So when I returned home, I asked him to meet me on the terrace and excitedly told him what had happened and how Rohan had proposed.

Karan gave a fake smile and congratulated me by hugging and went downstairs towards his room. I felt quite strange at his behaviour but ignored him and decided to celebrate the happy turn of events (But, still somewhere deep inside my heart, I wanted Karan to be with me, by my side, as it was the most wonderful moment of my life).

Rohan and I managed to complete all the preparations for our marriage (scheduled within a few days). In fact, Karan also helped us in the effort. I had mixed feelings for him (It was good that he was helping us, but I felt bad too, as I knew how he might have been feeling), but I wasn't able to express it, or do anything about it.

The D-day was inching closer. Events started unfolding two days before the marriage. Karan's family performed all the rituals & customs with lots of enthusiasm. Their warmth and affection made me feel so special, that I started wondering whether my parents could have ever given me even a fraction of what I received from them.

The night before my marriage brought on a strange unease. I wasn't able to sleep properly at all. Everybody pacified me that it was nothing but the stress associated with the event, but their explanation did not contain my restlessness.

Somewhere deep in my mind, I was thinking about Karan. I saw everyone else in the gathering except Karan. I searched for him everywhere but could not find him.

I did not realise when I dozed off, while brooding about Karan.

The next day, I got dressed in the beautiful bridal outfit. Not finding Karan anywhere, I found my mind in conflict with my heart. I paid heed to my heart's voice and impulsively chose to run away from the scene in search of him. I was worried about him.

My mind prompted me not to head into marriage with Rohan. I simply ran outside, away from the gaze of the people assembled there.

I didn't know where he was. I even tried calling him, but he didn't answer my calls.

I went to the ice-cream parlour (where we used to meet). He wasn't there either. I sat there and started crying.

Suddenly, someone came from behind and held my shoulder. I turned back and saw Karan standing behind me. I couldn't resist. I held him tightly and started crying. He was trying to stop me from crying.

We gave each other a smile and I confessed to him that I loved him truly and would never ever leave him. He also repeated the same vow, in reply.

What happened thereafter barely warrants any further elucidation.

What is important is that Karan and I are happily married and are living happily with our family and kids in the city of Kanpur – ***the place, where it all began; the city of love, life and passion!***

• LOVE THY CITY AS THY COMPANION •

PANKHURI MEHROTRA

"Who says I can't be free, from all of the things I used to be. Rewrite my history, who says I can't be free."

I sang along with John Mayer's honey sweet voice to get rid of the cacophony of voices in my head.

My phone beeped and I swiftly opened the message which read.

'Just reached *Phaphund!* The guy next to me says it would take another two hours from here.'

P.S: '*Phaphund!* Are you kidding me? My mother used to use this name for fungus on bread. Who keeps such a name for a city? Oh I forgot; anything can be expected out of *UPwaale*.'

I smiled and replied.

'Just like you can never write the post scripts shorter than the original text, similarly *UPwaale* can never get rid of their Desi names.'

Two more hours and then I would meet Aarav after a hiatus of over four months. When you are in a long distance relationship, there are just two kinds of days:

- The red lettered days when you meet your partner.
- The rest of the days when you just wish for the red lettered days to arrive.

Today was that day when I could show the middle finger to the second category of days.

Aarav and I had got into a relationship two years ago and since then, though we are separated by miles of distance on land, the distances between our hearts seems to have vanished. And in the words of my love, 'What's life and love without a bit of blood, sweat and pain. These pangs of separation will bear fruits of passion.'

I was lost in an era of reminiscence when suddenly a voice broke my bubble of thought.

'For your kind attention please. Train number 12034, Kanpur *Shatabdi Express* from New Delhi to Kanpur, is going to arrive shortly on platform no. 1.'

The ground beneath my feet started shaking (No, it wasn't because of the love effect but because the engine whistled past me). The coaches passed by me, one by one, till the time C4 coach halted right in front of me.

After a swarm of passengers got down I got a glimpse of him and my lips automatically curved into a smile. I rushed to wrap my arms around my world. He softly kissed my nape and whispered in my ears, 'Ishika, this is my first time in Kanpur and considering how everyone is staring at us, I guess people in this city aren't used to seeing such PDA.'

I jolted back as reality dawned and wiped a tear from the corner of my eye.

'Shhh!' Aarav held my face in his hand.

'I came here to meet my *UP ki gundi*, not this bone china doll who breaks down on just hugging me.'

'Shut up you liar, you said it would take you a couple of hours. How did you arrive at such jet fast speed?' I shouted regaining my *Lady*

Khali avatar.

He gave me a 'that's-like-my-brave-girl' punch and said 'I thought you would be dying to meet me. So to add a few more breaths to your life, I bribed the driver to drive the train at jet speed.'

We walked with our fingers entangled. I heard a man whistle and say something obnoxious. Aarav turned to see who he was but before he could react, I pulled him by his arm and said 'Leave it. When you are in UP you should ignore such mundane stuff.'

On reaching the parking lot, I folded my hands in a *Namaste* and began reciting in an air hostess tone.

'Welcome to Kanpur. This city was once famous for its leather products and high-ended industrialization, however, now-a-days it is in the news for being number one in pollution, dirt, chain snatching gangs, poor infrastructure etc. The weather is pleasant and cloudy with a slight breeze. If the traveller doesn't want the temperature to rise, he should refrain from commenting on any of the above said things. Otherwise the guide wouldn't hesitate in making things as hot as hell for him. If the traveller wishes to continue, he should nod.'

Aarav nodded between peals of laughter and said 'but what if?'

I placed my finger on his lips and started singing the song "*Baharon phool barsao, mera mehboob aaya hai. Mera mehboob aaya hai,*" as I showered rose flower petals on him.

'Ishika, what are you doing? Everybody is staring at us,' he said, laughter writ all over his face.

I ignored his blabbering and continued till his cheeks turned redder than the roses. 'You are in my city, so you have no other option but to walk my way, baby.'

'*Gunda Raj* at its best.' He said pointing at my dominance.

I slapped him and said 'Didn't my condition stick, Mr. Aarav? No commenting on anything.'

'Ouch!' he exclaimed.

'My touch-me-not; Get ready for the ride.' And with that I presented him our royal carriage.

'This!' he cried pointing at my rustic old scooty.

'Yes, your Highness. Kindly step up and make this ride a memorable one; one which would go down in history.'

'I don't know about history but I am sure this scooty can definitely make it to a historic museum.'

I turned and started moving to show my defiance.

'Sorry,' Aarav came behind me like a puppy. 'No more comments now.'

I pulled his cheeks and said 'This is why I love you so much.'

Both of us got on my scooty and we rode off.

'So where are we heading?' He asked, as I maneuvered through the heavy traffic outside Kanpur Central.

'The itinerary is set. You needn't worry about anything darling.'

'Now this, my dear boyfriend, is like the Old Delhi area.' I explained to him as we entered the busy Meston Road. 'You get good things at the cheapest price.'

'But why have they lined up all the vehicles in the middle of the road?' He questioned, seeing me drive with utmost difficulty through the heavy traffic.

'You see, that serves a dual purpose. Firstly, you needn't have to build a parking lot. Secondly, you needn't build a road divider because the vehicles act like one.'

'Great.' He applauded in admiration. 'How cleverly you mould things to save your city of shame.'

'Oh please, there is nothing to be ashamed of. I love every bit of my city. I feel a sense of belonging when I drive through these lanes and by lanes', I retorted back.

He listened patiently to all the stories I had to narrate to him - about the *beech-wala-mandir* and the mosque just adjacent to it, which had stood the test of time even during the riots; about the delicious *Hathras ke khasta* and *kachauries*, and the leather shops.

'And this is Cawnpore *Kotwali,*' I said, pointing to a dilapidated building covered under layers of green algae. 'They took a shot of this in *Dabangg*, I guess', I elaborated further.

'*Ahaan!* Don't remind me of that film Ishika'; throughout the movie my friends were teasing me - "Reconsider your choice, Aarav. *Kanpurwaali* doesn't seem to be a decent option".'

'Strike One.' I warned him.

'And this is the newest addition to the string of shopping malls in Kanpur.' I pointed to the Z-square mall.

'This one comes as a shocker. By the sheer size of it, looks equivalent to GIP or Select city walk.'

'Strike Two.' I patted him on his back.

'I am genuinely appreciating it. No undertone of sarcasm here,' he defended himself.

'And this is the Head Post Office.'

'I thought you never wrote a prem-patr to me because villages didn't have post offices. But after seeing this, I demand an explanation, Miss. Ishika.'

'Strike Three,' I admonished him lovingly.

'This is *Thaggu ke laddoo*. They have delicious *laddoos* and *baadaam kulfi*. You remember the song "*Aisa koi saga nahi jisko thaga nahi*" from the movie, *Bunty aur Babli*? This line is *Thaggu's* tagline, and a portion of it was shot here.'

'This is Naveen market, the favourite shopping destination for half of Kanpur. From shoes to hair clips, you name it, they have it.'

'But baby, this looks a lot different from the usual *gaon-ka-mela*.'

'Strike Four,' I said and applied the brakes.

'Is this the place where we are going to eat?' He looked puzzled.

'No, this is the place where we part ways, Mr. Aarav. Get down, right now.'

'Sorry, sorry, sorry,' he pleaded guilty and held his ear lobes.

I chuckled at his innocence and commanded like a dictator 'So you will zip it up from here onwards?'

'I promise,' he said; 'Unless I experience that uncontrollable urge, wherein if I don't speak, my lungs would burst.'

'I can grant that much leverage.'

I further showed him the place where the employees earned without having to do any work i.e. Kanpur Electricity Company, owing to the non-existent electricity supply in the city. Then I showed him the red building with broken glass windows and a clock tower which never displayed the correct time since its inception i.e. *Lal Imli*. For the first time his gob was shut when I told him about the century old factory and how it was a feather in the cap of the city.

'You look no short of a local gangster who is well aware of every nook and corner of his area. And, look at the way you are defiantly crossing the red lights despite the traffic cops standing. I am utterly scared', he squealed.

I laughed hysterically at Aarav's cuteness and replied 'Considering that you would ideally meld into one of those wonderful touch-me-not handsome guys to be kidnapped, I am planning to kidnap you.'

'This, my sweetheart, is the social heart of the city,' I said as we reached Arya Nagar. One can have great food here and enjoy great scenery as well.'

'Scenery,' he guffawed. 'You are right, considering the mountainous, rocky track we are traversing, it can well be counted as a hill station,' he said as we went through a roller coaster experience on the pot-holed road.

'You will come to know what I mean in a while' I said, as we stopped outside Aroma's to have a tummy-filling lunch.

'Though the shop is named Aroma's,' I said, as I munched on my Veg woofer burger, 'It serves as an eye tonic.'

'Eye tonic?' he gave a perplexed look.

I held his chin and turned his head to a gang of handsome hunks who got down from a tinted Fortuner which played loud music.

'*Tharki aurat*,' he commented.

'What is so perverted about it? When I was in school this used to be the hub for NSP. After coaching we used to flock here for both eye-candy and stomach filling candy.'

We finished our food and I took him to Veggies to have some salivary-gland tickling *paranthas*. He licked his fingertips till the last bite of the pasta *parantha* and declared; 'We are definitely booking them for our wedding.'

We continued our travel saga and I showed him one of Kanpur's hotspots, '*Pandit Maggie Wala*'

'It is a boy zone. No females allowed.' I explained.

'How come you know the details when it is a no-women's land?'

'Some things are not meant to be told, baby.'

'You bitch,' he pinched my waist and bit my neck.

'Ouch!' I cried. 'What are you doing Aarav; let me continue the drive, you stupid fool.'

We chatted on our way back till the time we reached Cantonment.

'From here we enter Kanpur Cantonment, where the twelve best years of my life were spent. Three of the best schools in Kanpur are located here.'

I narrated my school life memories as I showed him the schools.

'And here we enjoyed mouth-watering ice balls as we watched the boys from other schools perform bike stunts to impress the girls of my school. Those were some days. We used to jump on the mere mention of going to inter-school competitions, considering we would get some new topic of gossip.'

'Topic of gossip or topics to share comments like "ohhh, ahhh, he is so sexy".'

I hit him in his gut and continued. 'The next place we are going to, serves okayish food but the reason I come here is that it is far away from the hullabaloo of the city. The ambience... how do I tell you? Let us say if you are dying, the mere look of the place will add a few more breaths to your life.'

We were going through the motions of entering *Dhuaan*, when Aarav happened to catch a glimpse of the white walls and the blue upholstery; he said 'Now I get what you mean. It's like the light at the end of the tunnel.'

We sat down and had our brunch, after which we headed to one of the historic but forgotten places of the city. When we finally reached there, all Aarav had to say was 'Such a beautiful place can't exist in Kanpur.'

I smiled, held his hand and together we entered the All Souls Church.

What our eyes beheld was the great Gothic structure built after the first war of independence. The red sand stone building stood in all its might surrounded by the greenest of grass and trees.

We strolled around the perimeter of the church and then sat down beneath a tree next to the tombstones.

The silence was deafening and the peaceful atmosphere invigorated our souls. Somewhere afar, instrumental music was playing which added to the magic of the place. I slid a yellowish red box in Aarav's hand.

'What is this?'

'It's mandatory for every traveller to carry a minimum of 1kg of *Banarsi ke laddoo*. Otherwise, the T.T.E won't allow you to board the train and your relatives won't let you enter their house; Plus, I want to impress my 'to-be-in-laws'; and, *Banarsi* is the best way to woo anyone.'

A bright smile lit up his face and he said with gleaming eyes 'You are the best thing that has ever happened to me Ishika. How you take care of the minute details is spell binding.'

Aarav started playing with my fingers and said solemnly, 'Ishika, you know why I love you.'

I looked in his green grey eyes and said 'Why?'

'I love you because you are an original.' He said putting his head on my shoulder and kissing my palm. 'I always loved people from small towns. Metros were never of my interest. The way you people are so transparent, so honest in your gestures, I can bet it's difficult to find your species in Delhi.'

'That smile on your face when you were showing me the places. That sense of pride in your voice as you illustrated the details. I can never speak like that. To tell you the truth, I still rely on my GPRS to navigate through places in Delhi instead of my childhood memories.'

'I wish I could stay here with you like this, forever; sharing carefree laughter with my beloved, lifelong.'

'*Inshallah!* We will, Aarav; but for that, you will have to leave your family and become a *ghar jamaai*.'

We laughed, and how I wished our laughter continued to echo like that day… till eternity?

• LOVE AT FIRST SIGHT •

AMIT KARN

November 21st –

It was quite strange. A burst of rain in the afternoon, in the month of November was very unique especially for those who had been born and brought up in Kanpur. My family, Saurabh and I had reached one of the most famous places in Kanpur – the J. K. Temple at the scheduled time.

I cursorily checked my attire and appearance to reassure myself. We approached the temple through the garden. The soulful ambience and the serene surroundings of the temple took me down memory lane reminding me of that unforgettable incident which changed my life completely.

August 27th –

It was a regular August evening, cloudy and calm. My father who was working with the G. V. S. M Medical College had been allotted a new quarter. We had shifted from Type L to Type C quarter, just a few days ago. My mother was a regular visitor to the Anandeshwar temple and had hardly skipped any chance to visit it, but on that Monday evening she had felt unusually tired and asked me to go and offer prayers on her behalf. I agreed and called my best friend Saurabh, who lived on P. Road to accompany me.

He picked me up from my residence on his bike and both of us reached the temple in twenty minutes flat. On reaching the temple, we purchased prashaad and a milk sachet after removing our footwear.

We could reach the sanctum sanctorum of the temple after waiting for 10–15 minutes in the queue. As usual, it was a crowded evening in the temple. Lots of devotees were present and each one of them wanted to offer their prayers in a hurry. We somehow managed to find a place to sit and offer our prayers. While I was in the process of getting up and moving out, a full sachet of milk was poured on my head with the milk flowing all over my face. I was enraged and tried to find out the culprit. But before I could do anything, I felt a piece of cloth rubbing against my hair and face. I curiously raised my head to thank the person who was offering to help me in that situation when…

Oh! My God; I was taken aback at seeing the person. She turned out to be a thin fair complexioned girl around 22 years of age. Oh! She was damn gorgeous. I had never seen a girl as beautiful as she was. Those big dark eyes, sharp straight nose and rosy cheeks would have made anyone crazy. Those tiny ear rings, the cute little nose ring and a butterfly-shaped hair clip was adding to the magic enhancing her persona. She looked divine in her Indian outfit. To my mind, that dress appeared beautiful, because she made it look so. In a single line, she could have been termed 'poetry in motion'. It was then and there that I lost my heart. She kept saying 'sorry' and cleaning my face with her dupatta. I was dazed. Her fingers were touching my forehead. I lost my senses. She was anticipating my anger and there I was, sitting like a fool without uttering a single word. The crowded surroundings made no difference to the sense of utmost peace stealing over me.

It was when Saurabh shook me that I realized what was going on. Instead of scolding the culprit, I could only say, 'Thank you'. She smiled and said, 'sorry' one last time and moved away. Saurabh tapped me on my back and we came out of the temple, wore our sandals and headed towards the Parking.

The streams of the holy Ganga appeared cleaner and fresher that day. They were dancing to some celestial rhythm; just like my heart was beating to the rhythm of that divine beauty's heart. The sounds of the chants, the majestic panoramic view of the Ganga and the temple's spiritual ambience made me feel as though I was in heaven. Though I had been to this place many times it was only after this sweet accident that I realised how heavenly the place was.

Saurabh took his bike out of the Parking and we both proceeded home. All along the way my eyes were searching for that flawless beauty. I was thrilled; I had never felt this way before. I closed my eyes and tried to feel her touch again. I desperately wanted to see her again. I wanted to speak to her. I wanted to listen to her melodious voice. Saurabh happened to notice my smile, while I was immersed in my own thoughts. He started teasing me, to my enjoyment. I wanted him to talk more and more about her.

A few minutes later, we reached Bada Chauraha and found ourselves stuck in a traffic jam. Saurabh crossed the road when the signal turned green and reached the auto stand. I saw that same girl sitting in an auto! I asked Saurabh to immediately stop the bike and pointed towards her. Saurabh quickly took stock of the situation. On my prodding, he left me alone and hurriedly zoomed away with a knowing smile on his face.

I sat in that auto without knowing its destination. This was one of the craziest things I had ever done. I did not know why I was behaving like I did. Mama's boy was for the first time doing something without Mama's knowledge. The girl, with whom I had the loveliest accident of my life just half an hour ago, was sitting right in front of my eyes. I could not believe my own eyes. Was it real or was I dreaming? I was bemused. No, it was not a dream. I was excited. I was trying to watch her from the corner of my eyes, but she caught me doing that and I skipped a heartbeat or two. But a few seconds later, she smiled and I felt relieved. For the first time probably, I felt my heart beating really fast. I was in a totally different state of mind. It was for the first time that I was experiencing something like that. Was it love? I was surely in love, if it was – Love at first sight! I had heard a lot about it but never thought that one day, I too would fall prey to it. I was so happy and content at that moment that I started dreaming about her, draped in a saree. I started visualizing my surname after the initials of her name. I kept on clicking hundreds of her images in my eyes. Love was very much in the air, but well ensconced in the auto too.

It had become dark. I came to know from my co-passengers that the auto was heading towards Gumti No. 5, a destination just opposite the place where I lived. An otherwise painful auto ride emerged as an utterly enjoyable experience. The auto driver had been playing some typical desi songs like 'tum to thehre pardesi, saath kya nibhaoge' and then I suddenly realized that all those moments were not going to stay for long. In the next few minutes, she would probably step down and go to her place. I would never get a chance to see her again. I would probably never be able to tell her about my feelings. That fear of losing her made me bold and I decided to follow her when she would alight from the auto.

She got down from the auto at the Eighty Feet Road and I jumped out after her. She somehow sensed the situation and started taking long strides towards her place. I followed and went close to her and mustering all my courage together, stood in front of her.

I was shaking. My legs were trembling. I was feeling awkward. Somehow I started the conversation:

Me – Hi! What's your name?

She – Sorry, I don't know you and don't want to disclose my name to a stranger.

Me – Okay, don't tell me your name but can we become friends?

She – Why should I be friends with someone I do not know properly?

Me – Well, actually I do not know whether it is right or wrong, but I love you. I want to spend the rest of my life with you.

(I had never thought even in my wildest dreams that one day, after seeing a girl for a few minutes, I would follow her up to her home and propose to her while standing on a public road).

She – Are you nuts? Do you realize what you just said? Do you even know my name? And for your information, I am not that kind of a girl. My family would be very angry and upset, if they saw me talking to a stranger on the road. So please don't bother me and just go away.

She quickly left the scene. I could not say a single word in reply to her; rather, she barely stayed any longer to bear or hear me respond. I kept watching her going far away, until she completely disappeared from the scene. I was still standing there, motionless, not knowing what to do. I was sad, completely heart broken and felt like crying. A few tears could barely be held back from rolling down my cheeks. My cell phone rang suddenly and I picked up the call; it was Saurabh. He queried about my whereabouts and about 'her'. His every question thereafter sounded irritating to me. I cut him short curtly; I did not want to discuss the matter any longer. My world had been destroyed even before it had taken shape. Love at first sight was nothing but an illusion, it seemed.

I began to remain very distracted after that temple incident. I was feeling sad and lonely. My mental peace was lost. I had no reason whatsoever to be happy. The whole world seemed to have become a void in the absence of that girl.

I visited Anandeshwar temple many times after that day but did not see her even once thereafter. The same streams of water in the holy river Ganga appeared polluted and the same surroundings of the temple seemed to be noisy. How could a single person have made such an impact on one's life? She was not with me physically, but she seemed to be everywhere – in my dreams, in my thoughts, in my talks, in my heart, and in my soul. My heart was beating only because of the desire to meet her again. I was wondering why God made me meet her, when she was not a part of my destiny. People go to the temple in search of peace and happiness and there I was brooding, without love, happiness and mental peace.

Saurabh could not bear my pain any longer and told everything to my parents. My parents' were already in search of a suitable girl for me and coming to learn of the incident, they speeded up the process. They found it difficult to get the right match initially, but after a few weeks they found a few suitable alliances out of which they short listed three.

The first two girls we saw could not impress my family, which made me even more tense and depressed. I knew deep in my heart that whosoever would come, could never fill the void that angelic creature had left in my life. My family started preparing to meet the third and the last girl.

November 21st –

Saurabh tapped my shoulder and I was back again in the present. So there I was, preparing to see the third girl selected by my mother, deemed suited to be my wife. I was not interested and had been brought there forcefully.

The would-be bride's party was already present in the garden of the temple, but the girl had not arrived. We went there and seated ourselves. Formal conversations began between the parents of both the parties after they made themselves comfortable. Snacks and cold drinks were served by the girl's family. I was sitting on the ground when Saurabh signaled to me about the girl's arrival. The girl came with her sister and aunty from behind where I was seated. True to tradition, she touched the feet of all the elders of our family. Her parents asked both of us to talk freely and gave us much-needed privacy by disappearing from the scene. Saurabh too left us with a mysterious smile on his face. The girl was feeling shy and was sitting with her face held down. I had not seen her face yet. I went closer and asked her to raise her chin. She raised her face and as I saw her, I was shocked. My head started spinning. I could not believe my eyes. Was destiny playing with me? Was I dreaming?

Oh God! It was the very same fair complexioned thin girl who I had seen at the temple. The angel was sitting there right in front of my eyes just a few inches away. The girl who had virtually made me her slave in the very first meeting was feeling shy to even look at me. Those big dark eyes which once made me crazy were blinking in front of me. That face, which had once stolen my heart, was inviting me to see it again and again.

And by seeing me in front of her, she too was shocked and stunned.

With tears welling in my eyes, I held her hands and said; I know you are not that type of girl and I know I am nuts, but today after watching you talk to a stranger, that is me, your parents will not be angry and upset. So, I Amit, without even knowing your name, propose to you for marriage. I LOVE YOU. Would you like to spend the rest of your life with me?

And within a fraction of a second, my ears heard the most beautiful word ever, 'Yes'!

The skies took the cue from my moist and watering eyes; it started raining heavily. The Heavens too were probably celebrating our unison.

The ecstatic feeling was yet to sink in that this girl would share her life with me.. Her butterfly-shaped hair clip was assuring me that within a few days, she would in fact have my surname tagged after her name. I was going mad all over again. My dreams were turning true.

Saurabh came to see whether everything was all right and after seeing both of us together, he too smiled with tears of joy.

It was no longer a dream or mirage. Love at first sight did happen and bloomed into wedlock!

• NOTHING IS FORGOTTEN •
NEERAJ KUMAR NIGAM

I completed my schooling followed by graduation in Kanpur in 1977. I nurtured the fond hope that an industrial town, as renowned as Manchester for its innumerable textile mills and rightly labelled "Cawnpore - The Manchester of India" then, would not only provide me with lifelong employment, but would also allow me to find a reason to continue. My dreams however were short lived.

Closure of textile mills, IEL Plant, Singh Engineering, jute mills and several other industrial enterprises, small and big, led to mass retrenchment causing large scale unemployment. Kanpur's growth prospects and its future were in doldrums due to the industrial sickness that had spread like cancer. The writing on the wall was loud and clear; persons with job aspirations, particularly those who were in their mid-careers seeking growth or on the verge of starting their careers had no other choice but to quit Kanpur and look for outside employment to fulfill their livelihood concerns. The ones, who remained in Kanpur, were the unfortunate aged few who were at the end of their careers, lacking the zeal and the courage to venture out for a living.

I worked in a textile mill until 1994 and was constantly on the lookout for better jobs, but they were few and far between. Kanpur industry's remuneration levels were abysmally low, insufficient even for maintaining a simple, middle class family lifestyle. One could find only such kind of people in low salaried employment that either had family constraints or were saddled with financial liabilities. Their compelling family circumstances were exploited by greedy businessmen who utilized the cheap manpower to fill their coffers leading to large scale under- employment.

I considered myself fortunate to have got a job then at Lucknow to work for a Chennai based company in such a dismal scenario. LML Scooters India enterprise had been set up as a new enterprise promising gainful employment to the locals. Its closure within a short period of time was indeed shocking news, which depressed me a lot. Similar was the case with several other industries which came into existence, seemingly for availing the tax holiday, when the UPSIDC and UPFC developed the Rania and Jainpur industrial areas as tax-free zones to promote industrialization for generating employment. They disappeared the moment the tax benefits were withdrawn. The other traditional industries for which Kanpur was a name to reckon with in those days were the tanneries and the pan masala industries. These industries could not survive with the implementation of stricter pollution control laws by the state authorities in their sincere bid to address the genuine ecological and health related issues. The only trades in Kanpur which managed to stay afloat were the footwear and readymade garments industries. It had to console itself of just becoming a big trading centre for sarees in that part of the country.

My love for Kanpur saw me back there after 17 years; I'd taken up a job in a chemical plant in 2011. Within one month of my joining the plant, it was extinguished in an unfortunate fire accident. The same company however called me back to work in their new plant which they set up at Greater Noida later.

Consequent to my retirement in 2013, I am back at the place where I belong – Kanpur. I am back to square one – looking for a job commensurate with my experience to keep myself happily occupied!

It pains me to see the state in which Kanpur has landed itself – an industrial graveyard! I only hope that the entrepreneurial spirit of the younger generation would restore its past glory in a modern template, and it would not be required of us to remember Kanpur only as the "Cawnpore of the British!"

• AUTHOR PROFILES •

Ajay Mohan Jain is a B.Tech. from I.I.T. Kanpur and trained at I.I.M. Ahmedabad. He writes mostly on topics of general interest for various newspapers and periodicals including Economic Times, Hindustan Times, Femina, Data Quest, Computers Today, Jagran and has written a novel 'Nothing can be as Crazy...', published by Rupa & Co / 'Ek Banker Ki Romanchkari Kahani' (Hindi) by Prabhat Prakashan. The book has since figured twice in the bestsellers lists of The Hindu and India Today and is now available as an ebook.

Amit Karn is a mechanical engineer who is also a poet, writer, reader and cook. A believer in the magic of love, he can sacrifice money and wealth to spend his life with his loved one.

Bhavika Mathur is a restaurateur by profession. She likes to write stories and poetry. Writing has been her passion since childhood and she hopes to become an acclaimed author someday.

Deepak Khattar runs one of the oldest dry-cleaning firms in the country. He is a keen collector of antiques, stamps, first-day covers, coins, and more. The basement of his house, also his den and hideout, is a beautiful museum of his collectibles.

Fatima Mahmood writes English poems, short-stories and is currently working on a novel. Writing has been her passion since school days and she wishes to pursue writing as a career.

Jaikishan is a pen name of a leading businessman who wishes to keep his identity undisclosed.

Monika Pant is a writer from India and has had her short stories and poems published in several anthologies around the world. An English teacher for over 15 years, she also writes course books in English Grammar and literature for students. Her real life snippets are published in the 'Chicken Soup for the Indian Soul' series and a short story written by her was long-listed for the 2013 Commonwealth Short Story Prize.

Mukul K runs a start-up multimedia company. He is an independent filmmaker and has worked on many national and international films, TV series and documentaries. His book Get the Facts Photography, has been published by Scholastic India.

Neeruj Nigam is an AIMA member with 34 years of experience. Prior to retiring as the CEO of a multinational company at Greater Noida, Neeruj worked with the Elgin Mills Co Ltd (A Government company), J.K.Synthetics and T.T.K.Healthcare limited.

Pankhuri Mehrotra is currently pursuing CA but fiction books interest her more than study material. She is a firm believer of the saying 'Live Life to the Fullest'.

Paroma Sen is a professional content and creative writer with several years of experience in the field. She works for advertising agencies, web designing firms and content oriented firms on contractual basis providing consistent content support.

Rishabh Patel is currently pursuing his graduation in Science. Besides writing, he has a keen interest in reading, music and photography.

Printed in Great Britain
by Amazon